Lesbian Secrets

A sexy collection of hot and steamy lesbian erotica stories for girls who love girls

Claire Elliott

Table of Contents

Emma and Mila

"Yeah, baby, give it to me," Emma moaned as she held Mila's head between her thighs and against her dripping pussy. Emma bucked her hips up and cried out before collapsing on the bed. Breathing deeply as the cold night air swept in through the open window, Emma lit a cigarette and held Mila in her arms.

"I got so lucky," Emma said, inhaling deeply and exhaling to the side. Mila snuggled into Emma's large breasts, the same ones she had lovingly sucked and teased an hour earlier.

"I guess you have to go soon, hey, baby?" Emma said. She looked down and kissed the slender girl's body, her Caribbean skin smelling sweet and warm. Mila just nodded her head. Out of all the women she had been with that day, Emma was undoubtedly the most beautiful and gentle.

Mila had been nervous about Emma's intentions with her when she first came to her room. The tall, broad-shouldered woman monstered her, and as she had stood in the doorway and welcomed Mila.

"Is it wrong that I don't want to go," Mila whispered into Emma's ample cleavage, making Emma smile.

"Well, how about I just steal you away?" Emma teased but stopped smirking when she saw Mila's hopeful young eyes look up at her. Putting out her cigarette, Emma rolled Mila onto her back and ran her hand over the top of Mila's forehead. Bending her head and kissing the girl on the tip of her nose, Emma smiled as her thick blonde hair fell to the side, held back by the hands of the girl she had made love to for the last three hours.

"I better go," Mila said, her eyes begging for love she didn't believe would ever be for her. Emma dropped her hips onto the smaller frame of the girl under her, pinning her to the bed.

"Spread your thighs," Emma said in a husky voice, her eyes commanding Mila into obedience.

"There's a good girl," Emma praised, making Mila roll her head back in pleasure as Emma traced her fingers up and down the girl's still wet slit. Parting her lips, Mila felt Emma's tongue dominate her mouth. Wrapping her other arm around Mila's body, Emma broke their kiss just to kiss down her neck, giving Mila goosebumps.

"Can I go in here, sweetheart?" Emma asked, making Mila laugh.

"You can do whatever you want, that's kind of the point," she replied, pushing her hips forward only for Emma to pull her hand away.

"Well, I am a gentlewoman, that's kind of my point, princess," Emma replied, watching as Mila squirmed in her strong arms and looked away.

"Do whatever you want," Mila said, blushing and trying to pin Emma onto her back.

"I don't think that's going to work, sweetie," Emma smirked as she watched Mila's desperate attempts to keep her feelings out of their transaction.

"Come on, come to me," Emma said, sitting on the bed and pulling Mila into her arms once again but this time holding Mila's head to her chest as she began to cry.

"I know, baby girl, I know," Emma said. This wasn't the first girl who had cried after Emma had fucked her; she had that effect on women, and as much as she would have loved to have taken Mila with her, she knew she had to leave her behind. Emma worked for an online marketing company and spent her time traveling around the world due to the nature of her profession. She knew she wanted a girlfriend but had long ago settled for beautiful girls for a night because she just couldn't see how a typical girl would fit into her world. Most of the girls she had dated wanted her to stop traveling, to find a home base and settle, working from home, and hanging out with the same group of friends every weekend. That was not the life Emma wanted, in any capacity. She wanted to be in Paris for a party and then Milan for an art opening.

She wanted to fly to Germany for a holiday in the mountains and then Spain for the summer. She needed to experience the world. She craved it. Her high flying, champagne-style gypsy lifestyle was not something she was willing to compromise on, even if it meant that she had to settle for women for a night.

"When will I see you again this time?" Mila asked. The last time she had seen Emma had been a year ago, the time before that, it was two years. If she had been honest with herself, she had stayed in the game for the off chance that Emma would come back for her, but she didn't know if that was something she could keep waiting for.

"I don't know, honey," Emma said, enjoying how Mila's body silhouetted the crisp white bedsheets in the moonlight.

"I will admit, it is harder and harder to leave you," Emma said, pulling Mila onto her lap and holding her close. Mila buried her head into Emma's neck and sighed contently, letting herself melt into the older women's body and allowing herself a moment of solace.

"I'm coming with you," Mila said, nodding her head, taking Emma by surprise.

"Before you start," Mila quickly added before placing her hand over Emma's mouth, making her laugh, and her eyes soften.

"I have savings. You won't have to pay for me, and we can see how it goes, and if we hate each other then cool, I'll leave and go find something else to do with my life. But right, now, I can't let you leave me again," Mila said, biting her lip and taking her hand away from Emma's lips. Emma looked at Mila. Her phone begins to ring with the number of some other client.

"Do you need to get that?" Emma asked, tilting her head towards the side table where Mila's phone vibrated. Mila just shook her head and continued to stare intensely at Emma, who, in all her years, had never had a girl so invested in being with her.

"Let's give it a go then," Emma said, laughing as Mila squealed and wrapped her arms around Emma's neck, pulling her body onto hers and kissing her deeply. Falling back onto the bed, Emma parted her thighs, letting Mila's body fall between them before wrapping them around the girl's body.

"Now you can," Mila whispered into Emma's mouth. Puzzled, Emma raised an eyebrow and looked at Mila blankly.

"Touch me here," Mila explained, taking Emma's hand and placed it between her thighs and pressed it into her wetness. Pressing Mila's body to hers with one hand, Emma slid her finger into Mila's tight pussy, making her inhale deeply as Emma wrapped her legs around Mila's and forced them open.

"Dance on my fingers, baby girl," Emma instructed, watching Mila grind sensually up and down on top of Emma's soft voluptuous body. Pushing another finger into Mila only to make her cry out as she was stretched, Emma lovingly kissed the woman riding her with stamina.

"Come for Mama," Emma said, pulling

Mila's thigh into her own pussy and ran it up and down the young girl's thigh muscle, coating her in her juices as she dropped her hand onto Mila's ass and gripped it firmly. Emma forcefully fucked Mila's body with animal ambition as Mila cried out and shuddered as her pussy juices dripped down Emma's hand and wrist. Emma pulled out of her and grabbed Mila's thigh with both hands as she fucked herself against her body. Mila steadied herself by placing her hands on Emma's tits and bent forward to tease her nipples, biting them gently and sucking them, flicking them with her tongue as Emma rubbed her clit against her quad muscle.

"Let me. I want to feel you," Mila said, taking her hand and sliding three fingers into Emma easily, making her moan and roll her head backward as she closed her eyes.

"Fist me, angel," Emma instructed, making Mila smile excitedly as she closed her smaller hand into a fist and pushed it inside of Emma's eager pussy. With the feeling of being filled to capacity,

Emma shuddered as she came hard, reaching down to hold Mila's hand inside of her.

"I'm not done yet, darling," Emma said in a husky voice, desperate for more. As her orgasm subsided, she rolled her hips forward and backward, smiling as she saw how her hips hypnotized Mila, who began matching her movements.

"Oh god, baby girl. There it is, good girl," Emma moaned as she flipped Mila onto her back and ground down hard on the girl's fist as cum spilled from her pussy. Wrapping both her arms around Mila's body, Emma humped her feverishly as she came again, this time squirting hard and covering Mila's body with her juices. Mila kissed Emma passionately as she felt safe in the arms of the woman she had just destroyed with sexual exhaustion. Mila pushed Emma off her slightly, pulling her hand from Emma's dripping cunt, making her body squirt again.

"Are you done yet?" Mila teased, lighting a cigarette for Emma and placing it to her lips, her head nodding in response.

"You are perfect," Emma sleepily replied as she inhaled and held Mila close. Emma smiled and closed her eyes as the sun began to come up over the ocean's horizon making the water look like diamonds.

"I leave in a few hours. How long do you need to tie up everything here? I guess I could wait a little while longer if you need it?" Emma said, looking down at the near sleeping Mila in her arms.

"I only have to pack and get tickets to wherever we are going. I don't have any family that I need to say goodbye to, and friends are kind of the same," Mila replied, her head growing increasingly heavy on Emma's large breast. Nodding, Emma let Mila fall asleep in her arms as she watched the sunrise over the water, excited about the future could now hold.

Judy and Lisa

Judy and Lisa had been together for ten years. They had met at a lesbian event in their local area and had both fallen in love at first sight. Judy had worked in real estate, selling homes to the rich and famous, and Lisa worked in the banking sector. Their life had been a whirlwind of luxury and comfort, with both women enjoying the independent lifestyle their careers delivered while happily coming home to each other at the end of the day. But that was ten years ago. Today, while their careers are still in tack, their relationship does not resemble the passionate, loving, and sensual dynamic they fell in love with.

"Morning, babe," Judy absently said as she kissed Lisa's cheek on an average morning. She walked to the coffee machine, took the espresso that Lisa had routinely made and left waiting for Judy. Lisa waited until Judy was sitting on her high backed egg-blue upholstered lounge chair and began to scroll through page after page on her tablet.

"Judy, we need to talk," Lisa said, causing Judy to give her her undivided attention.

"Oh, this sounds unpleasant," Judy replied, putting her tablet down and finishing her coffee. Lisa just smiled bashfully and looked down to the marble floor.

"Things have been, well, lacking lately. Don't you think?" Lisa asked, hoping that she wasn't the only one feeling that lack of luster in their relationship. Judy sighed and pulled a face before looking back up at Lisa and nodded her head.

"I thought that it would just pass. But it's not, is it?" Judy replied, shaking her head and placing her head in her hands. Lisa sighed and crossed her legs before passing Judy a flyer she had picked up earlier in the week.

"What do you think about this for an idea?" Lisa asked as Judy read the flyer.

"Yeah, of course, we could go," Judy replied, making Lisa give a sly smile.

"I thought it might be fun to see if there was a girl we might want to take home," Lisa suggested, making Judy turn her head to look Lisa in the eye.

"Wow. Really?" Judy asked as Lisa nodded her head. The topic of a threesome had come up before, but Lisa had always turned it down, saying she didn't want to see Judy controlling another woman in front of her. Judy was dominating in bed, whereas Lisa enjoyed a more submissive approach, and Lisa had been worried that Judy would enjoy controlling another woman more than her.

"But I thought you weren't interested in that," Judy questioned, making Lisa laugh.

"I'm more, not interested in losing you, and if this is what our relationship needs to spice it up again, then I think it's something I want to try,"

Lisa replied. Judy's phone alarm sounded, signaling that she needed to leave for work.

"I've got to go. And baby, you wouldn't lose me, but you are right, we need to do something to make this more fun again. Let's give it a go, and if we hate it terribly, then we will just kick her out and try something else," Judy said before kissing Lisa on the lips and leaving for work.

The party was all they had been thinking about, and as Lisa had predicted, the thought of bringing another woman into their bed and excited them all week. They had stayed up talking about the type of woman they would be interested in, coming to a compromise on looks and personality. Lisa had made it a point of saying she wanted a younger woman, someone that she felt comfortable controlling, and Judy had agreed willingly, stating that she would prefer a blonde with an athletic figure. Both had agreed to a woman with a girlish charm and big tits, and they had fucked every night with a passion they had forgotten they had as their conversations had sparked a fire within each of them.

When the day of the party finally came. Lisa arrived home before Judy and went straight into the bathroom and began showering. She shaved, plucked, and cleaned her body and hair before stepping out of the shower just as Judy walked into the bathroom.

"Hi beautiful, you smell amazing," Judy said, kissing Lisa on the mouth, her tongue tasting Lisa's minty breath. Lisa blew dried her hair as Judy undressed slowly in front of her.

"Don't try to tease me, I'm not getting back into the shower with you, I'm already dry," Lisa said as she read the wicked gleam in Judy's eye.

"No fun," Judy replied, stepping into the shower and turning the warm water on. Lisa watched as Judy ran her hands over her body, cupping her tits before letting them bounce from her hands as her fingers snaked down to her pussy.

"I thought you had somewhere to be?" Judy

teased as she saw Lisa suck the bottom corner of her lip.

"Oh, shut up," Lisa just laughed back as she snapped out of her daze and went to their bedroom to get dressed. She put on a black lace thong and bra, admiring how her deep red manicure and pedicure complimented her lingerie. Her black strappy heels came next, and she poured herself a drink of whiskey, taking it in one gulp before turning back to find Judy standing in the doorway. Lisa quickly inhaled as she saw Judy in her emerald green lingerie, her thick black hair falling in waves down her back.

"Get on the bed," Judy instructed, looking at Lisa the way she had missed.

"And if I don't," Lisa replied, wanting to make Judy work for her tonight. Judy raised an eyebrow and casually walked over to Lisa before grabbing her roughly by the back of her head and pushing her over to her desk. Judy bent her over and pinned her down, still taller than Lisa, even though Lisa was wearing heels.

"Did it sound like an option, darling?" Judy said, kicking Lisa's feet apart and pulling the crotch of her panties aside.

"Oh, little kitten, I've missed this," Judy said, cupping Lisa's hot, wet pussy. Judy brought a hand around to Lisa's mouth and covered it as she dropped her body weight into Lisa's back to keep her down before pushing two fingers into Lisa's pussy, making her scream.

"Shh, shh, that's not what good girls say when they get something so nice happen to them. Say thank you, baby," Judy whispered into Lisa's ear, making her moan as her pussy covered Judy's fingers in her cream.

"Thank you, Judy," Lisa panted before Judy covered her mouth once more as she began fucking her bent over girlfriend on her desk. Pumping her fingers in and out of Lisa's pussy, Judy knew she was close, but deciding to deny her, Judy pulled out and repositioned Lisa's thong against her wet slit.

"That's all for now," Judy said, making Lisa

moan in frustration and roll her eyes. She had forgotten how mean Judy could be.

They continued to get ready, Lisa putting on her little black dress with a plunging V neckline, that dress had never let her down. Judy decided she would wear tailored trousers and a blouse, her beige heels matching the black pants and beige shirt with their signature red soles.

"Ready to go, baby?" Judy asked as their driver pulled up to the drive. Lisa nodded as she grabbed her silver clutch and headed towards the door.

"I didn't think there were any female drivers, let alone one that looked like that," Lisa whispered as she and Judy sat in the back of the car as they made their way through the city.

"I guess we just got lucky. A little like what you are about to be," Judy said as she winked to Lisa, who looked at her curiously. Before Lisa could clarify Judy's meaning, Judy was unbuttoning her trousers, revealing that she was wearing their strap-on.

"Judy!" Lisa hissed as her eyes grew wide.

"Come and suck it," Judy instructed, grabbing Lisa's head and pushing her mouth down on the cock that stuck out from Judy's pants.

"Good girl," Judy said as she felt Lisa open her throat and take it. Judy reached down Lisa's back and pulled up her dress, pulling her thong into her ass, making it jiggle.

"Yeah, I like that," Judy said, pushing up and deeper into Lisa's mouth. Gagging on the cock Judy was fucking her mouth with, the driver turned around at a stoplight to see where the noise was coming from.

"You girls look like you are having a fun night. I'm a little bit jealous," she said, driving away from the light as they turned green. Judy pulled Lisa's head up and tilted her head toward the driver. It was true. The driver was attractive. With blue eyes and blonde hair in a neat bun, her body was athletic, but she was in no way the damsel in distress that they had thought up in their brainstorming sessions the previous week.

Lisa smirked and nodded her head before sitting back in her seat and waiting for Judy to do something.

"You don't need to be jealous, you might need to park somewhere a little more discreet though," Judy said before grabbing Lisa's hair and pulling her back down onto the strap-on. The driver drove to a dead-end surrounded in trees in a quiet part of town before Judy let Lisa off her cock.

"I hope your jaw doesn't hurt too much, sweetheart," Judy said, rubbing Lisa's face with her thumbs before the driver came into the back seat. She had already put the driver and front passenger seats down to make the car feel like one big bed as she locked the door behind her. Before another could say another word, Lisa had sat on Judy's lap, giving Judy all the permission she needed as she began lifting Lisa's dress up to her thighs, pulling the wet crotch of her pants to the side and filling her to the hilt with the strap-on. Lisa bent forward and kissed the driver on the lips, moaning into her mouth as Judy began to pump in and out of her pussy, making her pussy lips stretch around the cock.

"Take your hair out," Judy instructed the driver who willingly obeyed, making Judy roll her head back and let out a moan in sexual relief and continue to fuck Lisa.

"Unzip her dress," Judy said, closing her eyes as she felt the strap-on harness push against her own throbbing clit as she fucked Lisa harder.

"Keep her bra on. I want you to watch her tits as you play with yourself, get naked for me," Judy commanded, feeling her orgasm building inside of her. Lisa was a moaning mess on Judy's lap. She had already had two orgasms, but Judy was not interested in letting her come down from them and instead continued to use her.

"Baby girl, you're getting fucked tonight," Judy whispered into Lisa's ear, driving her wild and making her begin to twerk on Judy's lap.

"There she is, my desperate, horny little slut," Judy said, slapping Lisa's thighs as she bounced on her lap. The driver had taken her clothes off, her body toned and eager as one hand played with her perky breast, and the other stroked her clit.

"Open your pussy lips, I want to see you," Judy instructed, waiting and watching as the driver obeyed.

"Touch her," Judy whispered in Lisa's ear, kissing her neck and cheek as Judy pushed her forward as another orgasm ravaged through Lisa's body. Lisa's hand roamed over the driver's body, sucking on her nipples as Judy positioned herself behind the bent-over woman and began pounding into her again.

"Reach between her thighs and finish her off," Judy instructed the driver as she pulled out of Lisa and began rolling a condom over the cock. The driver smiled, knowing what would be coming next.

"Yes, Ma'am," she said, watching as Lisa's eyes grew wide with the touch of another woman slowly entering her. Judy sat back and watched the two women begin to play. Lisa, on top of the driver, the driver's arm wrapped around Lisa's body as her other hand finger fucked her, rubbing on her clit and bringing on another shattering orgasm. Judy smiled as she watched her girlfriend collapse on the driver in exhaustion before gently pulling her off her and cradling her in her arms.

"I think you need a little rest, princess," Judy said affectionately before kissing Lisa as she had all those years ago. Lisa nodded and contentedly sighed as she settled onto the driver's seat and watched as Judy looked at the driver as though she were prey.

"Come here," Judy said, almost aggressively. She grabbed the driver's legs and pulled her to her strap-on, holding it in her hand as she rubbed the tip of it up and down the driver's slit making her moan.

"Oh, you like that. Well, let's see how much of it you can take," Judy almost growled as she pushed the tip in passed the driver's pussy lips and forcing her to take it deep inside of her.

"Open that pussy up to me," Judy barked as she slid out only to thrust in more forcefully, smirking as she felt the driver submit and relax against her.

"That didn't take long," Judy said as she began to plow the driver's cunt. Lisa reached out and ran her hands up and down Judy's body, kissing her lovingly before sitting on the driver's face, facing Judy.

"You better make me happy," Lisa said, making Judy smirk and lean forward to kiss her passionately as she fucked the driver who was fucking her girlfriend. Lisa slapped the driver's tits, pulling on her nipples as the driver's tongue entered her dripping pussy.

"Suck it, don't be a little bitch," Lisa said, slapping the driver's breasts, making her scream.

"That's it. Good, just like that," Lisa said, turning Judy on as she watched her girlfriend control another woman for her own pleasure. Pounding faster, Judy came just as the driver did, Lisa rubbing her clit and getting herself off at the same time. Slowly, Judy pulled out of the driver, Lisa gently got off her too, and the three of them sprawled out over the car seat in exhausted bliss.

"When you can, I think you should take us home," Judy said to the driver as she held Lisa in her arms, kissing her softly on the lips.

Sophie and Cleo

Cleo had worked for the same company for the last five years. She had managed to keep her position when the company merged, and she had even secured one a company car, one far nicer than anything her salary could have bought. She went to work, went swimming on a Friday afternoon, and rock climbing on the weekend. By all accounts and purposes, her life was great, and yet, she knew something was missing.

"Good morning Cleo," a man in a dark navy suit said, causing Cleo to look up from her computer screen. Cleo noticed the older woman immediately. With her stylish office dress and high black heels, her blonde hair held back in a loose but tidy bun, Cleo knew what this woman would be doing without the man having to tell her.

"This is Sophie. She will be replacing Kerry. I trust that you will show her around," the man in the navy suit said before smiling at both women and leaving. Sophie looked to the empty cubicle behind Cleo and then turned back to Cleo.

"Oh, um, yeah, sorry. That's where you'll be. Did they tell you why Kerry left?" Cleo asked, getting up and gesturing to the empty office chair.

"No, they didn't. But I've heard whispers," Sophie replied, beginning to take her possessions out of the box.

"Mental break down. The job just got to her," Cleo softly said.

"Where you two close?" Sophie asked, seeing the sad expression wash over Cleo's face. Nodding, Cleo went back to her side and turned around to once again face her computer screen.

The weeks went by with Cleo and Sophie developing a working routine. Sophie would pick up coffee from the lobby for both of them in the morning. Cleo would cover for her when she was late coming back from lunch, which was more often than not.

"I'm going to be late back today, babe," Sophie said as she placed Cleo's coffee cup down next to her.

"Aren't you always?" Cleo laughed, taking her cup in her hands and warming them. It was the middle of winter, and although the holidays were fast approaching, there was still a mountain of work to be done.

"No, I mean, like an hour late," Sophie said, patting Cleo on the head. This was something she had taken to doing recently, and Cleo had hoped that Sophie wasn't aware of how it made her clit tingle.

"Oh. Ok. Are you alright?" Cleo asked, spinning around in her seat and looking at Sophie with concern.

"I will be," Sophie said before winking at Cleo and spinning her chair back around.

"Now get on with your work," she casually said, making Cleo thankful she had spun her chair around as her face burned red at the command.

Cleo thought all day about what it was that Sophie could be doing, and as the hours ticked by, she began to grow increasingly worried that she had not returned. By the end of the day, Cleo had just taken to telling people she had gone home sick, but the knot in her stomach with worry would not settle. As 6 o'clock came around, Cleo decided that she better head home as well and resigned to the fact that she would just see Sophie tomorrow.

What if she got mugged on lunch or something? Cleo anxiously thought as she walked down the street. She pulled her coat tightly around her. The air was crisper than she had been prepared for, and she shut her eyes tightly against the wind. Bumping into something, she suddenly opened her eyes again and gasped as she saw Sophie standing in front of her.

"I thought something had happened to you," Cleo involuntarily said as she wrapped her arms around Sophie and hugged her. Laughing,

Sophie returned the embrace and ran her hands down Cleo's back. Breaking the hug, Cleo took a step back to see where they were.

"Um. Did you just come out of there?" Cleo asked. The brothel sign in bright pink reflected on the snow on the sidewalk. Sophie just bit her bottom lip and raised an eyebrow.

"And if I did?" Sophie asked in a way that made Cleo wish she hadn't challenged her. Cleo just shrugged her shoulders and looked away.

"Yes, I did. I see a girl every few days. I love sex. Do you have a problem with that?" Sophie asked, enjoying the discomfort she was layering on top of Cleo. Cleo just exhaled and shook her head, blushing and trying to begin walking once more.

"Oh no, you don't. You're coming with me little miss," Sophie said grabbing Cleo's hand and beginning to walk the other way. Cleo tried to suppress her smile, but as the older woman controlled her, she felt herself give in most enticingly.

"I've seen the way you look at me, I know

what you want pretty thing," Sophie said as they reached her car. Sophie held the door open for Cleo and watched as she got in before walking around to the drivers' side.

"Lift up your skirt," Sophie instructed as she began to drive away. Cleo hesitated, resulting in Sophie placing her hand on Cleo's thigh and moving the skirt up roughly.

"I said lift it up," Sophie repeated, placing her hand on Cleo's soft mound, making her squirm.

"So warm, so soft," Sophie said more to herself than Cleo as she stopped at a red light.

"Pull your tights down, move your panties to the side," Sophie instructed. This time, Cleo didn't hesitate. She obeyed Sophie, who rewarded her by stroking her fingers up and down Cleo's wet slit. Cleo moved her hips forward, making Sophie laugh.

"Greedy little thing aren't you," she said, pushing her fingers into Cleo as the light turned green. Keeping herself inside of Cleo's tight young pussy, Sophie drove on, rubbing Cleo's clit with her thumb and stealing glances at the younger woman writhing with sexual frustration in the seat next to her.

"God, you really are just so beautiful," Sophie said pulling up to her apartment building and driving underground to the parking lot. Sophie turned the car off, took her seat belt off, and in one quick motion pushed Cleo's seat down and that she could climb on top of the girl.

"Spread your thighs for me," Sophie sensually whispered into Cleo's ear. Obligingly, Cleo obeyed Sophie's command and felt Sophie begin to finger fuck her, pulling out of her aching cunt just to fill her back up again and again. As Cleo felt her orgasm nearing climax, Sophie smiled and began kissing her, groping at her breasts and feeling Cleo flood against her hand. Moaning in surrender, Cleo bucked her hips against Sophie's hand, wanting more, the need she had not having yet been satisfied. Sophie pulled away, fixing Cleo's panties back in place and wiping her hand clean over the top of them before pulling her tights back up around the smaller girl's waist.

"Time to go, princess," Sophie said, opening the car door and unbuckling her belt. Sophie got out on the other side and watched as Cleo timidly stood by the car.

"Come here," Sophie said, reaching for Cleo's hand and hold it tightly as she walked fast into the elevator. Pulling Cleo in and holding her tightly as the elevator doors opened into her penthouse suite, Sophie walked out into the space and laughed when she turned around to see Cleo looking around somewhat bewildered.

"I own a little bit of real estate. This one is my most recent. I take it that you like it," Sophie said, slowly taking off her clothes and letting them drop to the floor.

"Yeah, it's really lovely," Cleo said as she watched the woman in her 40's begin to walk over to her in only her lingerie and heels. Cleo's mouth dropped as she saw the older woman's fit body. Her muscles defined under her soft figure, her large breasts making Cleo swallow hard.

"Um," Cleo said, rubbing her arm and looking around. She liked the feeling of being lost in this woman's world. It made her feel strangely safe to be the desire of such a powerful woman.

"Shh. Get on your knees," Sophie said as she gently ran her fingers through Cleo's long brown hair. Without never breaking eye contact, Cleo bent her knees and watched as Sophie positioned herself over the top of her.

"Open that pretty little mouth of yours," Sophie instructed, watching as Cleo silently obeyed.

"There's a good girl," Sophie moaned as Cleo instinctively began licking between Sophie's pussy lips, sucking on her clit and pushing her tongue into the older woman's pussy, tasting her at her source.

"Just like that," Sophie said as she held Cleo's head firmly to her, pressing herself against the younger woman's mouth. Cleo flicked her tongue over Sophie's clit, sucking and teasing her as she felt Sophie bend her knees and begin grinding on her face. She could feel Sophie's juices start to drip down her chin and neck and knew that she was close.

"Look up at me, I want to see those beautiful big blue eyes," Sophie panted, moaning as Cleo's eyes were on her in an instant. Sophie looked down at her, kneeling on the floor, her cunt filling the girl's mouth, her eyes full of obedience and innocence.

"Fuck yes, angel," Sophie moaned as she exploded into Cleo's mouth, her cum spilling from Cleo's lips and dripping onto her crisp white button-down.

"I guess you won't be needing this anymore," Sophie said, stepping back and watching Cleo still kneeling on the floor.

"Come here," Sophie said, holding out her hand to Cleo. Cleo took it and stood, her knees giving way and stumbling.

"I've got you," Sophie said, wrapping her arm around Cleo's waist and helping her walk to the bathroom.

"Let me take care of you. That's what you want, isn't it, sweetheart?" Sophie said as she began to unbutton Cleo's blouse. Cleo nodded her head, forgetting for a moment the things she did to herself. Gasping as she felt Sophie's hands on her sides, Cleo jumped back from Sophie's reach and tried to cover up the scars on her sides.

"I think I should go," Cleo said, grabbing at her blouse, which Sophie still held.

"When did you do that to yourself?" Sophie said, overpowering Cleo and pulling her in close and holding her tight.

"Since forever," Cleo said, breaking down and crying into Sophie's chest. Sophie held her tight and kissed the top of her head.

"Why?" Sophie asked as she pulled Cleo into her lap and sat down on the heated bathroom tiles. Cleo just shrugged her shoulders and buried her face in Sophie's ample cleavage.

"Well, I guess that you are going to tell me when you tell me," Sophie said as she held Cleo into the night.

Cleo stayed the night at Sophie's, wrapped up in her arms Cleo had never felt safer or more content, and she knew that this was what she had been searching for for so long.

"Good morning, baby," Sophie said as she opened the curtains and let the sun stream into the room. Cleo blinked her eyes open and smiled sleepily at Sophie as she climbed back into bed. Cleo immediately snuggled into her soft loving body and contently sighed as Sophie wrapped her arms around her.

"So, why do you go to brothels?" Cleo asked Sophie. Sophie took a sip of her coffee she had placed on her nightstand before answering, finding the questions amusing.

"I love sex. I could have sex all day every day. But it's hard to find a partner who can keep up. So I go there because it doesn't matter if I tire them out," Sophie replied, placing her coffee cup back down on the night table. Cleo thought about her answer and knew that now Sophie would want her own questions resolved.

"Why do you cut yourself?" Sophie asked, pulling the sheets off Cleo and inspecting her body. Sophie gently touch the risen scar marks before pulling the sheets back around Cleo.

"It has just become a habit. I started when I was a teenager, going through a few rough things, it helped me to feel something, and now, it's just my go-to method of calming down," Cleo replied, shrugging her shoulders.

"Well, how would you feel about finding a new way to deal with your stress?" Sophie asked. Cleo looked at her peculiarly before slowly nodding.

"Good. I want to condition you to eat my pussy when you are feeling overwhelmed. If this is a power and control thing for you, I will happily give you power and control over my body. I think it could be a win-win," Sophie confidently said but frowned when Cleo shook her head.

"No?" Sophie asked, not many people said no to her and the times that they had she had not handled well. Tensing her calves, not wanting to loose Cleo, Sophie waited.

"I want to be more to you than just your release. If we are going to do this, I'd want to be your girlfriend, or whatever," Cleo said, feeling herself become shyer as her sentence went on.

"My girlfriend?" Sophie questioned. It had been a long time since Sophie had a woman to call her own, and she was surprised that such a young beauty would want to be tied down to her. Sure, she knew that she looked great for her age, but the 15 year age gap was still there.

"Yeah, I mean, you said you knew what I wanted, I guess you didn't know as much as you thought you did," Cleo laughed.

"Oh I knew, I am just surprised that it's still what you want. Come here," Sophie said, kissing Cleo full on the mouth. Cleo opened her mouth and felt Sophie begin to explore her with her tongue, making her moan into the kiss. Sophie flung back the bedsheets and climbed on top of Cleo, pinning her wrists above her head and forcing her knees apart with her thigh.

"You feel so good," Sophie moaned as she let Cleo's wrists go and began to trace her hands down her body. Over the mounds of her breasts, she was squeezing them as they filled her hands. Stopping at her panties, Sophie gently rolled them down off Cleo's hips as she spat on her hand and began rubbing Cleo's pussy, cupping her firmly as her fingers parted her pussy lips. Cleo wriggled and moaned as she was taken, making Sophie smile at her accomplishment.

"Such a beautiful girl," Sophie said as she pushed her nipple into Cleo's mouth and silenced her moans.

"Suck," Sophie instructed as she began to slide her finger into Cleo's tight pussy. Feeling her muscles tighten and contract around her finger, Sophie pushed another in, forcing more of her breast into Cleo's mouth as the girl gasped and moaned at the intrusion.

"Are you going to be a good girl for me, Cleo?" Sophie asked, almost hypnotizing Cleo as she said her name while she was taken. Cleo just nodded her head as she suckled from the other woman, bringing her hands up to hold her breast, the weight of it causing her biceps to flex. Sophie just smiled as she moved her fingers inside of Cleo, making her buck her hips. Sophie laughed and placed her hand on top of Cleo's pelvis, enjoying how she felt her fingers inside of her pushing out her little tummy with each stroke. Cleo just moaned and rolled her eyes back in her head as she was held still and fucked, her orgasm flooding her body, only making Sophie fuck her harder.

"I'm going to teach you to hold off cumming, but for now, little one, have at it," Sophie said, but Cleo hardly heard as another intense orgasm shook her body. Pulling out of her, Sophie got up and walked to her cupboard, pulled out her strap-op, and began harnessing herself up.

"Do you know where I am going to put this?" Sophie said as she jerked the black rubber cock, which stood proudly out in front of her as she walked back to Cleo. Cleo just shook her head, and as she began to speak, Sophie pushed it into her mouth.

"I'll just show you then, shall I?" She questioned, pushing it further into Cleo's mouth.

"Breath, baby. Open your throat to me," Sophie loving instructed as tears ran down Cleo's eyes from her reflex. Sophie pulled out, so just the tip was in Cleo's mouth as she waited for Cleo to catch her breath. Slowly, Sophie pushed herself back in, stopping when she saw the tears well back up in Cleo's eyes.

"Such a pretty girl," Sophie cooed, reaching out and rubbing Cleo's cheek affectionately.

"Looks like I have a few things to teach you," Sophie said as she pulled her cock from Cleo's lips and flipped her onto her stomach. Cleo tried to get on all fours, but Sophie gently slapped her ass and held her down in the middle of her back with her hand.

"Stay," Sophie instructed as she grabbed at Cleo's ass and spread her cheeks open.

"Sophie I," Cleo said in a panic, not wanting

to be fucked in the ass. Sophie let her hand slap Cleo's ass, making it go red instantly.

"I'm not going to fuck your cute little ass, baby," Sophie said as she pulled Cleo's hips up slightly and pushed the tip of the cock passed her lips and pushed the tip into her pussy. Gasping, Cleo wriggled as she was held up, Sophie waiting until she stopped before pushing herself further into the young woman's cunt. Holding Cleo's hips to her body, Sophie watched as Cleo's back slunk down, the curve beginning to glisten with sweat. This is what Sophie had been waiting for. It was in this moment that she knew Cleo had surrendered to her. Sophie pulled out of Cleo just to force herself back in, reaching down to take Cleo's hands and place them on her head as she began to fuck her passionately.

"Do you like that, baby," Sophie panted, feeling the harness of her strap-op rub against her clit.

"Fuck yes, don't stop, please don't stop," Cleo replied, her pussy squirting as she came.

Sophie watched as Cleo's juices coated her cock. She stopped, pushed Cleo to the bed, and began grinding on her, humping her with animal aggression as she edged herself.

"Come here," Sophie moaned as she pulled out of Cleo, ripped the harness off, and pushed Cleo's hand into her cunt.

"Fist me, princess. Fuck me good," Sophie said, rolling her head back and moaning in sexual frusteration as her need to cum gripped her body. Grabbing Cleo's wrist and fucking herself with it as she came, squirting out around Cleo's wrist and covering the girl in her cum. Sophie panted as she pulled Cleo close to her and felt her cunt leak into Cleo's thigh.

"I think this could work out really nicely," Sophie said, stroking Cleo's hair and kissing her cheek as she closed her eyes.

"What are you doing?" Cleo asked as she groped at Sophie's breasts.

"Sleeping," Sophie replied, opening one eye and looking at Cleo.

"Not yet you aren't," Cleo replied as she wriggled out of Sophie's embrace and began sucking on her clit.

Hannah and Sasha

I am so happy I am coming home to you. Work is such a bore. I honestly don't know how much longer I can be bothered going. The people are so rude and disrespectful. The clients are even worse. I have signed until the end of the year, and being someone true to my word, I will stay there until then, but everything about that place is just so basic I can not stand it! But coming home to you is lovely. The cozy little love nest that we have made for ourselves is like something from a luxury country home magazine.

I pull up into the driveway and smile as I see your car already there, I hope you have already put the fire on, it's one of those rainy days perfect for watching movies and drinking hot chocolate all wrapped up in cuddly blankets while the fire burns. The crackling sound of burning wood and the smell of hot embers filling the air as our marshmallows melt.

"Hello, gorgeous," I say as I find you in the bathroom. Your body is so beautiful. The tattoos of your teenage years on your back and shoulders changing slowly as your body matures into your thirties. I have loved watching you change and grow. From the wild party girl who did cocaine mixed with alcohol and cigarettes every weekend to a woman who now only buys cashmere blankets, I must say I have loved every version of you that you have explored.

"Hi. I didn't hear you come in," you reply as you turn around and see me standing naked by the entrance of the shower watching you. When you and I designed this house, we decided doors on the shower were pointless, and as I walk into the warm water, I stand under the rainwater showerhead and let the water fall over my body. I open my eyes and take a step back, running my fingers through my hair and blink at you. You are looking plainly at me as though you've never seen anything as magnificent as me and take my hand in yours.

"Sasha," you say in your low husky voice. I smirk, this is my favorite mood to be in with you, when the week just slips off my shoulders, that nothing else is as important as you and me in the shower. That the outside world holds zero consequence to us.

"Hannah," I reply, playfully.

"Yeah, come here," you say as though my reply has given you the confidence and permission you were looking for to act out whatever illicit act you have been pondering. You pull me in and hold me tight, the warmth of your large breasts against mine, making me moan as you lift my chin to kiss your wet mouth. You kiss tastes like the mints you chew all day to stop you from smoking again, and their sweet tastes makes me want to kiss you more. You sit down on the floor of the bathroom and place me on top of you, sitting on your lap facing you as you kiss down my neck. You lean back and squeeze my breasts, flicking my nipples until I am squirming on your lap giggling.

"I want to try something else with you tonight," you whisper in my ear, making me giggle again.

"Well, ok, we've done it before obviously. We've done most things before. But do you feel like getting fucked with my strap tonight?" You ask. That's one of the things I love about you. You always ask me before you just go ahead and do something.

"Yeah. I want you to fuck my pussy with your strap baby," I whisper in your ear and smirk as you pull it from behind you.

"Where were you hiding that?" I ask as I get off your lap and watch as you put it on. I have always marveled at how good you look wearing it. You really do own it as you stroke it in front of my mouth.

"Open," you command, gently stroking my cheek and slapping my lips with the tip until I obey. You push into my mouth, making me suck you and take you deep in my throat until I am gaging.

"Such a pretty girl," you say as my eyes water. You pull out of my mouth and sit back down, pulling me back onto your lap as I was before, but this time your strap is between us, sticking up and waiting.

"Get on it," you say, lifting my ass cheeks up, making me rise before you let go and drop me onto your cock, filling me and making me let out a moan as it spears my tight hole.

"Shh, take it little one," you say leaning forward and stroking my wet hair as you push it further inside of me. I hadn't realized that it could be so deep as I feel the harness rub against my clit, making me moan in pleasure.

"There you go. Hold on, baby," you said as I wrap my arms around your neck and feel you slide down the shower wall before you buck your hips up and make me begin to ride you. I have always loved how strong you are. Some women I guess, could be intimidated by you, but I find your strength so sexy. I love knowing that you can take care of me in every way. I ride you, feeling your hands on my ass as you pound me, my clit getting flicked by the harness. I can feel my orgasm building deep inside me, and I know that I am going to squirt so hard against you. Maybe this is why you wanted to do this in the shower. You turn me around, and I lean forward to grip your shins as you fill me from behind and continue your onslaught. How I love how you fuck me and smile as you moan as your own orgasm hits you, making you fuck me harder.

"Yes baby, oh god, yes," you moan as you finish just as I squeal and cum with you. You made a good call about fucking in the shower, and I feel my pussy juices squirting around your cock and drip onto you and down my thighs.

"Did you like that beautiful?" You laugh as I almost slip on the shower floor as I pull you from my tight pussy. I nod and come to cuddle next to you and spread my thighs, letting the water wash away the mess. The water hits my clit so wonderfully, and I moan and close my eyes as I lean into you and let the water get me off again.

"Always such a pretty little slut. You love it, don't you baby girl," you whisper as she let you hand fall onto my pussy, and I feel you begin to circle my throbbing clit. I bite my bottom lip and try to suppress a moan as I roll my head back and close my eyes. Your fingers feel like velvet rubbing me ever so gently, making me squirm as you wrap your legs around mine, forcing me to keep them open. I loved how you do this, it's like you know exactly what to do to drive me over the edge.

"Where do you think you are going, pretty girl?" You tease as your other hand begins to grope my breasts as your other fingers become coated in my cum, my body falling limp in your arms. You release me, kissing my body and making me frustrated before you turn the water off before picking me up and carrying me to our bedroom and helping me dress. I am always so tired after we have sex, and I love that you don't ever seem to mind.

"Hannah, you are perfect. I love you so

much," I say sleepily. I feel you kiss my forehead before you get up and walk over to the fireplace, lighting it as I fall asleep.

Sally and Jess

"Sally, I'm home!" I call from the front door. When I got home from work and saw your car in the driveway, I was so excited that you were home early, I ran up the garden path and quickly opened the door. But I knew you wouldn't have heard me come in because I heard the shower running. I put my bag down on my special pink bag hook in our mudroom and kicked my wet boots off, placing them on the shoe rack just the way you like. I like that I can do the things that you have taught me without you needing to remind me to do them. Sometimes I really love being your good girl, today feels like one of those days. I giggle as I tiptoe to the bathroom, hearing you singing in the shower. I've never had a Mistress who sings in the shower before, and I sit by the door and listen to your songs. You're a surprisingly good singer. I was surprised when you first sang for me in the car ride home from our first picnic in the woods. I had pressed the window down, my hair getting windswept as I felt the air against my face, you turned the radio down and began to sing. Your song, making me blush and unsure of what to do as I sat quietly in my seat and listened. You looked at me several times during it, making me uncertain of what to say, so I just settled in and let you reach me with your song. I've gotten used to you suddenly bursting out in song since then, I've even found myself missing it when you've had a big day and don't have a song in your heart.

"Oh, little girl, I didn't hear you come in," you say, opening the door suddenly. I giggle, and you bend down to kiss me before taking my hand and leading me to the bedroom.

"How was your day?" You ask, making me roll my eyes. I hate my boring HR job in the city, but it gets the job done and pays the bills and then some, so for now, I've decided to keep it.

"Lame," I reply, not interested in telling you

about my boring day filled with boring people who lead boring lives. You smile, and I can see you have other things on your mind as well.

"Why don't you come here," you say, patting your lap as you sit down on the edge of the bed. I bite my bottom lip, surprised that you'd want to give me a random spanking but move to you as instructed. I hold my breath as I lay across your lap, hoping that I don't hurt you. Even though you are only a few years older than me, I still think I'm tougher than you and smirk as you grab a fistful of my hair and pull my head back.

"Lift up your skirt," you whisper, making my heart race as I reach behind and expose my emerald green lace thong. I can tell you like it by the way your hands move over my firm, full ass, feeling my wetness as you push my thighs apart.

"Such a pretty girl," you say, spanking my ass without warning. I force myself to stay silent, hoping that its what you want. For someone so open, I still struggle to feel comfortable and confident in my choices when I'm around you. It's not like you make me guess what you desire, it's just that I can't believe that you would genuinely want me, and I'd hate to lose you.

"You weren't expecting such a firm hand, where you?" You whisper, making me fall into your world immediately. I sometimes hate how easily you can have me. I hate that trying to fight you only makes me want you more, and I really hate that you know this.

"No, Mistress," I answer, knowing better than to make you wait. You rub my ass, groping at it while holding my head back, making me stare up at you, my throat stretching painfully. You can see my struggle, my eyes starting to water as I struggle to swallow. Coming down hard on my ass in several quick hits, you watch as I struggle not to break, kissing my forehead as my breaths come in shallow, labored breaths. Releasing my head, you slowly guide it back down just as I feel the blood surge through my veins, making me dizzy. You hold my head in the nook of your arm as I tense my strong muscular thighs on your soft body and fight my urge to snuggle into you. I know that you aren't finished your fun by the way you are running your finger up and down my wet, panty-covered slit. I suck my bottom lip, only for you to replace it with your thumb, correcting me when I slowly stink my teeth into it for fun.

"If you have to much energy, I'll give you something else to do," you say, making me try to hide my smirk. You pull my panties to the side and continue your slow onslaught, making me whimper in frustration. You were waiting for that, you like me on edge, begging for your touch.

"No, you're not there yet," you casually say, continuing to tease me. I want to have more of you, as I slightly buck my hips, wanting you inside of me.

"Don't be such a slut. You'll get what I give you," you say, making me groan in frustration. You've been working on this with me for a while now, teaching me how to stay still and quiet while you enjoy my body. I hate it, I secretly think that's why you do it, but I'm not sure of your motives.

Maybe it's just to have me accept something I don't want or to see how far you can go without a challenge.

You suddenly enter me with two fingers, curling them inside of me and stroking up and down my arching back.

"My little gymnast," you say as I stuck on your thumb and push my hips down on your hand.

"Come on, then, come and get it," you say, taking your thumb from my mouth and wrapping your arm around my neck as you push into me firmly, making me take you hard and fast.

"Don't make me wait," you whisper, pulling your fingers out just to slap my ass hard before shoving them back inside of me. I know what I'm supposed to do as I begin backing up onto your hand, grinding down on the fingers you have filled me with as your thumb begins to rub my clit, making me moan. You tighten your grip around my neck, bend down to kiss the top of my head before pulling out, just as my orgasm breaks and leaves me panting in your lap. I can tell you are smiling at me by the warmth in your voice.

"Good girl," you say, standing up and watching as I catch myself before I hit the ground.

"Just like a little pussy cat," you say, watching as my body contorts, the muscles of my toned arms, tummy, and thighs flexing in the subtle light coming from that hallway lamp. I move to stand in front of you, unsure of what you want me to do before you smile and reach out for my hand, pulling me to you.

"I love the way you look at me. So innocent, so sweet," you say, pulling me into your arms and holding me as I feel your heartbeat against your naked skin. I hold my breath, still finding your soft touch unnerving, wishing that I could let myself go and be with you the way you want.

"I'm not going to hurt you. You're safe here," I hear you whisper as my pulse races, wanting to believe you, but doubting you with almost every fiber in my body. I like that you are never offended that I don't just give you what you want. I love that you know I'm trying to and that you don't push too hard. I slowly look up at you, surprised that I'm still yearning for you with the deepest of desires when you hear your phone ring. I move away from you, assuming that you will answer it, only to be pulled back into you.

"What makes you think anything could be more important than you?" You say, a slight frown and loving smile appearing on your face as you shake your head in disbelief that I would ever guess your devotion. I just shrug my shoulder, my hair falling out from behind my ear and relax into you.

"There you go," you say, enjoying the vulnerability I am giving you, rocking me slowly as I fight myself to allow your love to last.

"What is it about me you find so exciting?" I ask you as we sit at the dinner table later that night. You have changed into your nightclothes. I can hardly call them pajamas. They are just navy sweat pants and a grey t-shirt. You look up at me over the tea you are now drinking and place it down thoughtfully. I've never known a person who drinks tea like you do.

"I like that you are so transformative. You can hold your own, for better or for worse. I like that you can be one person one moment but only need a gentle touch to become someone completely else, and I like the way you surrender to me. You're not submissive in a traditional sense, but you trust me with you, and I like having that control over you," you reply. I am a little shocked. I had just assumed you'd say something like, that you loved my tits or the way I could take a beating, but you see me, and I think it is because of that that I find myself constantly drawn to your side wanting to stay forever.

"Do you want my attention, baby girl?" You ask, looking at me with your unwavering stare. I shift uncomfortably under your spell, nodding slowly and looking up at you with the gaze you enjoy so much. You push your chair back and spread your legs, looking at me expectantly. I hope you're not going to make me lick your pussy. I really don't feel like doing that right now. Walking over to you, you snap your fingers and point to the ground, shaking your head, silently commanding me to crawl to you. I drop to my knees, grateful for the thick carpeted floors we have in our home as I feel my old skateboarding accident sends jabs of pain up into my knee. I try to hide it, using my foot to support my weight, but you notice everything. That's always been the annoying thing about you, you watch. You see past my front, past the guard, I put up and somehow always manage to pull the wall down, at times, much to my distress As I reach you, you place a hand down onto my head and wrap your legs around me as you continue to read whatever it is you are reading on your kindle. I sigh contentedly, nuzzling into you, and feeling your warmth. Your hand is stroking my hair, and as I close my eyes, wondering what kind of dreams I will have tonight. I have started to have really strange and scary dreams. Last week I woke you up because I was screaming in my sleep. I love that you never get annoyed by things like that. You just got me my some water and cuddled me into you, humming me a soft tune and kissing my forehead as I drifted off back to sleep. You start humming as you stroke my hair, twirling it in your fingers as I feel myself falling asleep against your thigh.

It's my favorite day of the week, Saturday! On Saturdays, you are always in such a fun mood because it's market day, and you love getting up early and heading off to the markets. I have often wondered why we have to go, but when I taste all the fresh, home ground food, I can't deny that it tastes 100% better than anything bought in the stores.

Today I woke up before you and spent half an hour watching the morning sunshine on your face. I run my fingers over your cheek, enjoying the contours of your sharp jawline.

"I am still asleep, baby," you say in your sleepy voice, making me giggle and get out of bed slowly, trying not to wake you up any more than I already have. I walk to the living room, knowing that my pot of tea will be ready for me, having been prepared by you the night before. I smile, seeing that you have also placed two almond and cinnamon cookies wrapped in my beeswax wraps next to the pot of tea. I boil the water and pour the water into the pot of tea, sweet-smelling tea.

"Come over here. I've got something special for you," you suddenly say, startling me and causing me to spill the tea I was about to take a sip from. The hot liquid spills onto the kitchen floor. I look at you with fear in my eyes as I try to clean it up quickly.

"It's alright baby, let me help you clean it up. I guess you were deep in thought, huh?" You say, making me relieved that you aren't mad. We finish cleaning it up, and you pour me a new tea and take a bite of my cookie. You have that wicked look in your eyes, which can only ever mean one thing, and I giggle, knowing what will follow your smile.

"I know that we would usually go to the market today. But, I thought maybe you wanted to stay in and play instead?" You say, making my eyes go wide. I can't hide the smile spread across my lips, and my eyes sparkle with excitement.

"Perfect, you whisper into my ear as you hold my head in your hands. I quickly take one last bite of my cookie, making you laugh as you watch me chew quickly.

"Get on your knees, princess," you say, gently slapping my face as I follow your instruction. You slowly peel off your track pants, taking me by surprise by you having no panties on.

"Stick out your tongue, darling," you instruct, smiling as I obey you. You move towards me, rubbing your clit and pussy over my mouth as I start to suck and lick your pussy.

"Good girl. Pretty little kitty," you say, placing your hand on my head and stroking my hair as you rub your pussy over my lips. I know that you love it when I stick my tongue into your wet hole, and as I lick deep inside of you, you moan and push me back harder against the wall. I taste your sweet honey beginning to drip against my lips, as I start sucking your clit and replacing my tongue in your hole with my fingers, quickly finding your g-spot.

"Don't you dare fucking stop," you breathlessly say. As if I would, having you at the mercy of my fingers, mouth, lips, and tongue is one of my greatest pleasures. I curl my fingers inside of you, making your legs start to shake. I know that you won't be able to take me teasing you for much longer, and I smile and breath into your pussy as I slow my movements down.

"I said not to stop," you growl, making me giggle.

"But I haven't stopped. See," I playfully say, slowly licking up and down your slit, making you moan in frustration and pull me to the floor before sitting on my face.

"Lick this pussy bitch. You should be so lucky this queen wants you," you say, grinding down onto my face, moaning as I obey you, and you feel my tongue back inside of you. You bend forward and reach into my pants, taking me by surprise. You part my pussy lips and spit on your hand before bringing it back down my pants and rubbing my clit roughly as I eat you out.

"Mmm yeah baby girl, eat that pussy. Worship Mama's cunt," you moan stuffing two fingers into my pussy and making me moan against your dripping pussy, making you begin to twerk on my face as you cum. You finger fuck my pussy with your fingers while your thumb flicks my throbbing clit, making me cum easily just as your orgasm fades. I tap your thighs urgently, and you laugh and lift off my face as I gasp for air.

"Oh baby girl, did I smother your little mouth with my queen pussy?" You tease coming to wrap me in your arms. I nod my head and cuddle into you. You adjust my pants and cradle me in your arms as I bite my bottom lip. I have always found sex to be so triggering after it is finished, and you kiss my forehead and rock me gently.

"You're ok baby. I've got you, you're safe here with me," you say as I wriggle out of your arms, pushing your hand away when you reach for me. I frown at you and can feel my breathing become ragged as I look at you angrily. I love that you know exactly what I am trying to say because most of the times, I don't know what I am trying to say.

"Oh, you wanna fight, hey, princess?" You say, standing up and pulling your pants back up. I smile and watch as you jump around and raise your fists like a boxer. I stand up too and wipe the tear that has escaped my eye away, throwing the first punch which you dodge.

"Oh, that pretty little left hook isn't going to get me this time," you say playfully, attempting to jab me. I make semi-gentle contact with you several times before I drop my arms and breath out in a sigh of relief.

"All good?" You ask, going into the kitchen and pouring two glasses of water. I come up behind you, wrap my arms around your waist, and kiss the back of your neck.

"Yeah. Thanks," I say happily. I love that you never make me feel weird about living with sexual trauma. It's weird still wanting to fuck you and be fucked but feeling weird afterward.

"You're my favorite person," I say, resting my head on your back and sighing happily.

Silvia and Julia

Silvia had always loved music. She had played in the school band and sung in the choir at church on a Sunday. When she had graduated high school, she had gone to college to pursue a career in the musical arts with high hopes of becoming an opera singer. That was until she met her roommate Julia on the first day of college.

Julia had come from the wrong side of the tracks, with a dry sense of humor and a glare that seemed only to fade when she was sleeping.

Julia was lying on the top of her bed when Silvia walked into the room with her suitcase and pillow.

"Hello. I'm Silvia. How are you?" Silvia asked politely. Julia just raised an eyebrow. Her raven black hair was sprawled out over her pillow, and her tattooed arms were crossed over her chest.

"Fine," Julia muttered, finding the polished Silvia instantly irritating. Silvia just faked a smile, something she had become increasingly good at with years of practice.

"Do you mind if I hang this up?" Silvia asked as she unzipped her suitcase and pulled out her framed poster of her winning her high school music award. Julia just sighed and stood up slowly. Silvia was surprised at how tall Julia was and looked down at the black combat boots that Julia wore.

"Look at me," Julia said, lifting Silvia's chin to meet her eyes.

"I don't what you do, where you put your things, who you bring back here so long as you don't go through my things. Ok, princess?" Julia explained, making Silvia blush and try to pull away from Julia's hand on her chin.

"Alright," Silvia replied quietly, her blonde hair falling out behind her ear and tumbling in its loose waves around her face. Julia smiled, the piercing in the middle of her bottom lip complimented against the dark red lipstick she wore. Julia turned to walk away, leaving Silvia feeling strange and almost breathless.

"I'm not a princess, by the way," Silvia said, suddenly feeling the need to have Julia's approval. Julia stopped as she reached for the doorknob, turning it and opening the door slightly before speaking again.

"Whatever you say, angel," Julia replied, winking at Silvia before she walked out the door and closed it behind her.

Silvia had shaken off her first encounter with Julia and, as the weeks rolled by, had enjoyed making friends with other like-minded people in her courses. Over lunch, she would write in her notebook under the big tree near her dorm building and would sometimes see Julia either coming home from a big night out or heading out for a big night. She had heard rumors about Julia, that she was in some sort of devil cult, that she was the local drug dealer on campus and that she was a lesbian. The other people in her course would make fun of her much to Silvia's distress, making Silvia wonder why she cared what they said about her.

"She's a freak. Like hello, combat boots, how 90's could you get?" One of the girls in Silvia's class said as Julia walked past their open classroom door.

"Maybe it's just her style. Anyway, it doesn't really matter what she wears, does it? Hey, did you do the homework?" Silvia said as she desperately tried to steer the conversation away from her roommate.

"I'm just saying. I would never be could dead in those kinds of outfits. Gross," the girl said, only stopping as the lecture began.
Silvia thought the time would never end as she quickly packed up her things and headed out of the lecture an hour later.

"Hey, we are all going out. One of the guys is going to get us beer. Want to come?" The girl who had made fun of Julia said to Silvia.

"Oh, no. It's ok, I don't drink," Silvia said, wishing that she hadn't the moment the girl gave her a disapproving look.

"Whatever," the girl said, turning around before Silvia could say anything else. Silvia dropped her head and walked slowly back toward her dorm room, feeling like the biggest loser in the world.

She opened her door and smiled at Julia, who was assuming the usual position of her arms crossed over her chest and lying on her bed, staring at the ceiling.

"How was class angel?" Julia said, more friendly than she had ever seemed. After several attempts to shake the nickname Julia had given her, Silvia had accepted it in defeat.

"It was alright," Silvia lied as she placed her handbag down next to her desk and sat in her desk chair facing the wall. Julia twitched her lips from one side to the other before standing up and walking over to Silvia and turning her chair around to see that she was crying.

"Oh, angel. What's wrong?" Julia said, sounding genuinely concerned. Julia reached forward and placed both her hands on the sides of Silvia's face and wiped her tears away with her thumbs before kneeling down in front of her and waiting for her to stop crying.

"They are just so mean. They made fun of you, and then when I said I don't drink, I got totally rejected. Like drinking is not the most important thing in the world, and who cares what someone wears or does or whatever," Silvia said through sobs. Julia just smirked, which made Silvia begin to cry all over again.

"Come on, Silvia, don't cry, angel. It's alright," Julia said, taking Silvia's hand and leading her to the floor. Julia rested against the end of Silvia's bed and pulled her into her arms, wrapping them around her. Julia was surprised at how well Silvia fit into her. Silvia pushed gently on Julia's shoulders as she began to stop crying and looked at her with her watery green eyes before suddenly kissing her on the lips.

"Woah, angel," Julia said, pushing her back and looking at her in surprise.

"I'm sorry. I don't know what came over me," Silvia said, getting up just to have Julia grab her wrist and spin her around and push her onto her bed.

"I do," Julia said as she stroked Silvia's hair back from her forehead. Silvia smiled and reached for Julia, who let her body drop and rest next to Silvia's.

"I didn't know you liked girls too," Julia said, making Silvia laugh.

"I don't think I like girls. I think I like you," Silvia said, making Julia bite her bottom lip and smile.

"Let me show you how much you like me," Julia whispered into Silvia's ear as she placed her hands under Silvia's loose t-shirt and trace her fingertips up to Silvia's breasts.

"Take your shirt off for me," Julia said, sitting up and leaning back on her elbows.

"Ok," Silvia said softly as she pulled her shirt off to reveal her toned young body and light pink bra.

"My little angel," Julia said, pulling Silvia onto her larger body and smiling as Silvia groped her breasts.

"They are bigger than mine," Silvia said, making Julia laugh.

"Thank you for pointing that out to me. I hadn't noticed," Julia said as she unhooked Silvia's bra with one hand and pulled it off her just as she became shy and covered herself up.

"Take your hands away for me," Julia said, pulling her band singlet off and unhooking her own red lace bra, exposing her breasts with her piercing bars through her nipples to Silvia, who just gasped.

"Do you want to touch them?" Julia asked, taking Silvia's hands in her and placing them on her large tits, squeezing them and making Silvia pull on her nipples.

"Did it hurt?" Silvia asked Julia, who just

shook her head.

"It felt like rough foreplay," Julia said, pushing Silvia onto her back and placing her body on top of hers. Silvia gasped as she felt the weight of another body on top of her and felt her pussy begin to tingle with excitement. Silvia bit her lip and looked away, embarrassed she didn't know what to do next, making Julia smile.

"Let me take the lead, angel?" Julia said to Silvia, who was already nodding her head and looking at her vulnerably.

"Just say stop. Better yet, red. Say red, if you want to stop alright? I won't think you are lame or silly or whatever horrible things you call yourself if you want to stop, alright?" Julia explained, making Silvia smile shyly and nod her head. With that, Julia lifted her hips off Silva and nudged her knee between Silvia's thighs.

"The first thing I want you to do is open your legs for me," Julia said, feeling Silvia obey her while looking at her with the most beautiful eyes Julia had ever seen.

"I'm going to touch you, here," Julia said, cupping Silvia's pussy and biting her bottom lip in desire as she felt the puffy pussy lips against her hand.

"And here," Julia continued as she pulled Silvia's panties to the side and touched her slit with two fingers making her jump.

"You're alright. Just breathe," Julia said as she parted Silvia's lips and felt her wetness making her moan. Julia smiled as she saw Silvia close her eyes and continue to moan as Julia's fingers stroked up and down her wet slit, circling her clit and making it hard. Silvia opened her eyes suddenly as she felt Julia at the entrance of her pussy and looked at her fearfully.

"I've never. Um, I don't," Silvia stammered as Julia moved her body to the side and stroked Silvia's forehead, kissing the tip of her nose and wrapping her arm around Silvia, rolling her into Julia's large tits.

"You're going to love what I do to you, angel," Julia said as she pushed one finger into

Silvia's tight virgin pussy, making her moan and try to push Julia off her.

"Shh, shh, just breathe baby girl. Mommy's got you," Julia said as she held Silvia firmly in her arms. Silvia looked up at her in shock at what she had just said, watching as Julia smirked and raised an eyebrow at her making her blush. Julia stopped moving her finger inside Silvia until she felt Silvia relax around her finger and felt the seal she wasn't sure if she should break or not.

"I'm not going to hurt you, little angel," Julia said, pulling her fingers back slightly and thumbing Silvia's clit.

"I don't want to do this anymore," Silvia said as Julia kissed her passionately.

"Are you sure?" Julia teased as she felt Silvia open her legs and push her pussy against Julia's hand.

"Maybe just a little longer," Silvia said as she felt Julia push another finger inside of her.

"Yeah, just a little longer, angel," Julia replied as she kissed along Silvia's neck as she began rhythmically curling her fingers inside of Silvia, who moaned and closed her eyes before rolling her head back and rocking her hips against Julia's hand.

"What?!" Silvia suddenly said, opening her eyes and frantically pulling away from Julia and sitting with her knees to her chest in the corner of the bed as she felt her pussy orgasm for the first time.

"Come back to me. You were such a good girl," Julia said, confusing Silvia.

"You just came, baby girl. That's what just happened to you," Julia explained as Silvia bit her bottom lip and looked distressed.

"It's kinda the point of all of this sweetheart. Come here," Julia said, opening her arms to Silvia, who crawled into her arms before Julia closed them around her and rocked her, kissing the top of her head as Silvia bit her cuticles.

"You kinda robbed yourself of that one. Can I give you another orgasm, darling?" Julia said to Silvia, who just shrugged her shoulders before nodding.

"I want to hear you say it," Julia said, spitting into her hand and rubbing Silvia's pussy, making her gasp.

"Yeah, I want to feel that again," Silvia whispered, reaching forward and steadying herself on Julia's thighs. Julia smiled and moved behind Silvia before pulling her back towards her. Julia parted Silvia's legs with hers, feeling how Silvia tried to put her thighs back together.

"No, baby. I want you like this," Julia whispered in Silvia's ear as she wrapped an arm over Silvia's body, holding her in place as she continued to stroke her clit and tease her pussy.

"Tell Mommy that you want it, angel," Julia said as she began to push into Silvia once more. Silvia ground her teeth together as she felt Julia push more forcefully inside of her. Biting her lip, she felt Julia slap her breast and pinch her nipple, making her squeal in pain.

"Shh, you don't someone coming in, do you? Let Mommy you want it," Julia said, repeating her instruction.

"I want it, Mommy," Silvia said almost inaudibly by making Julia moan and push past Silvia's seal. Silvia cried out only to have her mouth covered by Julia's hand, as she felt hot tears roll down her cheeks.

"Shh, it's done now, baby girl. It won't hurt for much longer," Julia said as she held Silvia and pulled out of her. Silvia saw the blood on Julia's fingers and gasped before turning around to look at Julia.

"Baby, you don't need to look so heartbroken. It's better that I do it than a gross guy who doesn't care about you. I care about you. I am the one who sees you and what you really want and need. I can keep you safe, angel," Julia said, kissing Silvia's lips and parting her lips with her tongue.

"So, what happens now?" Silvia said, pushing Julia back and breaking the kiss. Julia thought for a moment before she shrugged her shoulders.

"I guess, anything you want," Julia replied as Silvia stood up and groaned in pain. She doubled over and pressed against her uterus.

"I want you to take me to get a beer," Silvia said, reaching under her skirt and pulling her panties down and taking her skirt off.

"You're underage. You're only 19, baby," Julia replied, causing Silvia to raise an eyebrow.

"Since when do you care about rules?" Silvia said as she threw her blood-stained panties at Julia, making her laugh and roll her eyes.

"Fine. Maybe, a warm shower first might be nice, though?" Julia said, walking into their bathroom and turning on the shower.

"Come in with me," Silvia said, grabbing Julia's hand and pulling her into the shower without giving her a chance to take her clothes off. Julia smirked as the water washed away some of her make-up as she peeled her wet pants off. Silvia gasped as she saw the neatly trimmed but thick bush of black pubic hair Julia sported.

"I didn't think people kept it anymore,"

Silvia said as she reached out to touch Julia.

"It's coming back. But I kinda do what I want, and I like it, but I like my girlfriends shaven like you little angel," Julia said as Silvia looked at her thigh tattoos.

"Is that what I am. Your girlfriend?" Silvia said as she pushed two fingers into Julia's cunt, taking her by surprise.

"If you want," Julia breathlessly said as Silvia worked her the same way she had just been fucked.

"Oh, baby, quick learner," Julia said as she pushed against the shower walls and moaned as Silvia found her g-spot.

"Mommy, do you like it?" Silvia said, making Julia bend her knees to try to have Silvia deeper inside of her as she moaned in sexual heat.

"Yeah, Mommy loves it. Such a good girl for me," Julia moaned as Silvia brought her other hand onto Julia's clit and rubbed her hard as she came.

"Fuck!" Julia yelled as she grabbed Silvia's wrist and humped her hand as her cum dripped from her cunt. Silvia smirked as she took her hand off Julia's clit and slapped her face with it.

"Get on your knees," Silvia suddenly commanded, taking Julia by surprise.

"Did I stutter bitch?" Silvia said as Julia looked at her dumbfounded.

"Where did my sweet little girl go?" Julia smirked as she followed Silvia's instruction.

"You're about to see how sweet I am," Silvia said as she pushed her pussy onto Julia's mouth.

"Suck me," Silvia said, her gentle voice returning as Julia buried her face in Silvia's pussy. Sucking her clit and circling her tongue around, it was all Silvia needed until her body shuddered in orgasm, making her laugh as she felt Julia lap up her juices.

"Oh my god," Silvia said as she let go of Julia's wet hair and let her stand back up.

"I like this," Silvia said as her mind raced with a world she never knew existed.

"That's kinda the point," Julia replied, turning the shower off and reaching for Silvia's towel.

"Cute," she said as she saw Silvia wrap it around her and look at her with excited puppy dog eyes.

"Baby, can you get my stool please?" Julia called from the garage. Silvia and Julia had been together since that fatefully day in their dorm room, and four years later, they had both graduated and were now in a rock band with Julia as the drummer and Silvia as lead singer. They had become successful through uploading their videos to the internet and had been joined by three other members of the band.

"It's already on stage," Silvia replied as she looked out at the crowd that was beginning to come into the sold-out arena.

Maz and Eliza

Maz was the most stereotypical soccer coach anyone would have ever seen. She wore her long blonde hair in a ponytail under her green cap. Her short black shorts shirts always showed off her long tanned and toned legs after years of running. The long sleeve white shorts shirts she wore would always outline her newly done fake DD breasts and muscular biceps, and the colorful shoes she wore made her look like anyone's coach dream. Maz had been the coach of the Southern Vixens for the last five years after retiring from playing for the top league for female football. A welcomed coach, the women, had taken to her immediately, many of the players having started their sporting career after having Maz as their role model as they moved up the ranks. Eliza was one of those women.

At 25 years old, Eliza had been given her chance to play for Maz and the Southern Vixens after being scouted and drafted by Maz herself. Eliza had thought all her Christmases had come at once when she had put on the Southern Vixens jersey in the press release and felt the warming touch of Maz's hand under the table as Eliza answered questions from the various news reporters.

"Pass her the ball!" Maz yelled from the sidelines as Eliza run up their opponent's goal. Following Maz's instructions, Eliza passed the ball to her teammate, who sidestepped an opponent and kicked a goal making the crowd roar.

"Yes!" Maz yelled, pumping the air with her fist before switching Eliza over with another player.

"Why did you take me out!?" Eliza asked, horrified that she had been taken out of the last ten minutes of the second after of the premiership game.

"Because I want you rested. You're going on

after the next play," Maz replied as she watched the field as her team went through the motions of the same play and again scoring another goal.

"See, now go and do it again," Maz said as she slapped Eliza on the ass she passed and ran onto the field as her teammate came off the field. Again, the team scored just on the buzzer, and the crowd erupted as the Southern Vixens took out the win for the year. Their song came on over the speakings, and the girls jumped up and down and cheered until their faces hurt from smiling. Eliza looked over at Maz, surprised when she found her already staring at her. Eliza felt the crowd fade and held eye contact with Maz, who grinned at her before winking and turning away, causing Eliza to bite her bottom lip before joining her friends in celebration.

A week later, as Eliza was resting at home after several days of celebrating and tv and radio interviews, she heard a knock at her door. Getting up, she smiled when she saw Maz standing at her door with a six-pack of beer.

"I heard it's your guilty pleasure," she said as Eliza opened the door and welcomed her inside.

"You heard right," Eliza replied, taking the gift and leading Maz to the kitchen. She placed the beer down on the counter before turning around to find Maz standing close in front of her, her hands resting on either side of Eliza on the bench. Maz leaned down and kissed Eliza full on the mouth, tasting her with her tongue before breaking the kiss.

"Am I mistaken?" Maz asked as she ran her fingers through Eliza's chestnut brown hair. Maz cupped Eliza's face in her hands and place her thumb as Eliza's mouth and watched as she sucked it and closed her lips, making them pout before shaking her head.

"No," Eliza softly said as she wrapped her arms around the woman twice her age before standing on her tippy toes to kiss her again. Maz smiled into the kiss as she wrapped one arm around Eliza's waist and the other under her legs as she lifted her and carried her into the lounge. Placing her down on her back, Maz stood in front of her as she slowly pulled her shirt off, revealing her perfect body and full breasts in her black lace bra. Getting lost in the woman in front of her, Eliza tried to get up only to have Maz place her foot on her chest and push her back down.

"Stay," Maz instructed lovingly before taking her pants off to reveal a thick strap-on making Eliza's eyes go wide.

"Come here, baby," Maz said, reaching her hand out to Eliza, who crawled to her and knelt in front of the cock Maz was jerking slowly in her hand.

"Open your pretty little mouth," she said, watching as Eliza followed her instructions. Sliding the cock between her lips, Maz pushed the tip in and moaned as she saw Eliza's lips pout around her cock.

"So beautiful. I know you wore that pretty little dress just for me at the awards night," Maz said, pushing herself deeper into Eliza's mouth, happy that she opened her throat to her, taking her deeply.

"Good girl," Maz moaned as she saw Eliza's eyes start to water and slowly pulled out of her. Maz reached for the short pink cotton shorts Eliza wore and pulled them off, smiling when she saw that she wasn't wearing any panties.

"Dirty girl," Maz said before rubbing her wet cock up and down Eliza's moist slit, watching as Eliza turned around and bent forward. Maz watched as she pushed the tip into Eliza's tight pussy, watching how her body accepted the thick cock Maz wanted to fuck her with.

"Such a good girl," Maz said, pushing into Eliza slowly, smiling when she heard Eliza cry out and arch her back.

"Just a little more," Maz said, pushing into her hilt and holding her hips there as Eliza felt herself be stretched. Reaching around, Maz rubbed Eliza's clit as she pulled out of her only to push back in over and over until she felt Eliza relax around her cock and begin to take it.

"There's a good girl. Take my cock, baby," Maz said, grabbing onto both of Eliza's hips and thrusting aggressively into her as she moaned. Falling limp, Eliza felt her body being taken at Maz's mercy, sighing when she finally pulled out of her and came to lay next to her.

"Come here," Maz said to Eliza, who was slowly regaining her composure. Maz pulled the younger girl into her strong arms and held her shuddering body close as she felt Eliza's pussy drip cum onto her thigh. Eliza snuggled into Maz's breasts and began to cry.

"What is it, baby?" Maz asked, worried that she had hurt her.

"I don't know," Eliza replied, resting her hand on Maz's breast, circling her nipple as her tears wet Maz's chest as she held Eliza.

"Was this just sex for you?" Eliza said softly. Maz kissed the top of her forehead and thumbed her tears away.

"No," Maz replied, stroking Eliza's hair and feeling her melt into their embrace.

"Ok," Eliza replied, making Maz laugh.

"Ok?" She questioned to a nodding Eliza.

"I didn't want just to be sex. I want something more," Eliza explained as Maz kissed her tenderly.

"Tell me what you want, baby," Maz said moving when she felt Eliza shift in her arms.

"I want you to be mine," Eliza replied, feeling out of her depth.

"I know that you have a whole life and," Eliza began to say, getting cut off by Maz's kiss on her lips.

"Hush little one. Everyone has a life, but I want you in mine," Maz replied, smiling as she felt Eliza wrap her arms around her and fall asleep on her chest.

Eliza woke up the sound of music coming from the kitchen. She blinked her eyes sleepily as she looked around the room. The curtains were still drawn closed. The room was cool and dark. She stayed there for a moment, stretched out and yawned before slowly flexing her legs and arms and getting out of bed.

"Good morning, beautiful girl," Maz happily said as she heard Eliza coming up behind her.

"Hi," Eliza replied sleepily, rubbing her eyes.

"I've made you breakfast. Sit down. I want to talk about where this could go," Maz said, kissing Eliza on the forehead before turning back around. Eliza couldn't help the smile which came across her face.

Mine, at last, she thought as she watched Maz bring over pancakes and bacon.

Brittany and Jennifer

I'm Jennifer, 38 years old, and happily divorced for four years. The divorce had nothing to do with sex, it was great, but that was about the only thing. Since my divorce, I have vowed to enjoy life as much as I can, and I go out a lot to regularly meet other men. With how many men I have had sex within the last four years, I really don't know anymore. I always do it 100% safely, or nothing happens, safety is really important to me. Although, I have to admit that I have become a bit addicted to the one-night stands. But I keep setting the bar high enough so that I don't just get with anyone. In 7 out of 10 cases, I have even fucked with married guys. I do not care. I never give an address or telephone number, so it's never more than for the night. Rarely do I run into the man in question again. But there is always one exception. I forced him out of my mind for the longest time, but unfortunately, I couldn't keep lying to myself that I am in love with the boyfriend of my best friend, Brittany. They are both a few years younger than me, and I have often wondered how we all manage to get along so well. I dream of him; I would love to spend a night with him even if it was just one night. I just don't know if he, Jake is his name, is the kind of guy to cheat on his wife. I recently decided to venture out. To test how far I can go, to test whether he could be into me like am I him.

I invited Jake and Brittany to my house for dinner. We do that often, so there was nothing special there, and the night was filled with laughter as the drinks flowed. We played some drinking games, and as the night went on, we were all seriously tipsy. We talked about anything and everything. When Jake went outside to smoke, Brittany, and I started talking about men. Apparently, one of my last preys was a colleague of hers who was quite bragging at work about a new girlfriend of his. I told Brittany that she could make it clear to him not to have any illusions about the continued existence of a possible relationship. We laughed at how stupid men were that they believed that just because you spend time with them they think that you are going to be with them forever. When Jake came back inside, I told Brittany and him about my addiction to one-night stands.

I saw Jake looking interested when I told him how I am living my life and enjoyed his attention. They were both clearly unaware of this part of my life. As the evening progressed, we became more and more drunk. Brittany had to go to the bathroom, and that was the moment I was waiting for. A few moments only with Jake. I asked him for his opinion about my way of life. He said he found it exciting and was surprised to find so many married men would have a one night stand. I asked if he would be interested in that as his face turned bright red. With a slight crack in his voice, he said that he would consider it with me because I was his girlfriend's friend. He apparently trusted me that I would not tell Megan about what would happen between us, but he quickly began talking about something else when Megan returned. I wanted to raise the subject again and wondered if as many women would be unfaithful to their husbands as vice versa. I myself had never cheated on my husband in my eight-year marriage. I did say that my ex was a beast in bed, but he was not a nice guy, and it would not surprise me if he and regularly went to someone else.

I got comfortable with another drink and began questioning Brittany and Jake if they had ever had a threesome. Brittany and Jake listened to me, amused. The evening flew by, and it was time for Jake and Brittany to go home. When I said goodbye, I felt how Jake took hold of me more tightly than usual; I felt his hand caress my ass. As if it were by accident, I stroked his crotch. Fifteen minutes later, I received a text message — a number that I didn't know. It turned out to be Jake, who got my number from Brittany's cell phone. He wrote that I definitely had to come to their house again, even if Brittany just happened to be home.

Two weeks later, I thought I was going to see Jake and Brittany. Brittany and Jake had recently moved back into Brittany's parent's house after their lease was up, and she couldn't find an apartment that suited her. I saw Jake parked his car in the garage, but Brittany's car was gone. That could be because Brittany works on Saturday night every few weeks. I drove up the driveway and went to the front door and rang the bell. Nobody opened the door.

Strange, I thought, maybe they are gone together in Brittany's car. When I went around to the side door, it was open. I heard music, so I walked inside, and then I heard the shower.

Jake would not have heard the bell, I thought. For a moment, I doubted my decision to come but decided to put on my naughty shoes, or rather, to take off my real shoes and go towards the sound. Slowly I went up the stairs. The sound of the shower stopped, and then there was only music. I knew that if I went in now, he would be standing there naked. He would be scared, but based on the last text message, he might not mind. I opened the door and entered, my heart pounding like crazy. Just before entering, I had loosened a few buttons further down my blouse. And suddenly... there I stood... face to face with a naked... Brittany! After a brief scream of horror, she asked me what I came into her bathroom so unexpectedly, secretly, and unasked. I really didn't know what to say at the time. She looked at me from top to bottom and asked me if I came for Jake. I turned red. My best friend had caught me; I didn't want to lose her, not like this. Brittany soon calmed down. She came a little shorter and said she knew what I had asked Jake, his answer, and even the text. I wanted to apologize, but that was not necessary, she said. She told me that he had become so horny that night that they had great sex all night.

"Maybe I should thank you and Jake for

that," she said. She dropped the towel that she had started holding to her on the floor.

"Jake told me he would like to do something like that. But if you are going to fuck him, you're going to fuck me too," Brittany whispered in my ear. Immediately afterward, I felt her tongue against my earlobe. Her hand went inside my open blouse and slid quickly and easily behind my bra. She looked at me for a moment and then pressed her mouth against mine, her tongue pressed against my lips. Instinctively I opened my mouth, and before I realized what was happening, I was kissing this beautiful woman. I tried to shake the thoughts of fucking a woman from my mind and tried to push her off me, but she held onto my tight and kept me sitting next to her until I gave in and moaned into the kiss. I stroked her back and reached for her beautifully shaped ass. She unbuttoned my blouse and ripped at my clothes.

"Jake will come home soon. I want him to catch us like this," said Brittany. She kissed me again and then licked over my neck to my hardened nipples. Her hand rubbed between my legs as she went even lower. She sat down on her knees and started licking me the way I have rarely experienced. I opened my legs and felt her tongue make its way through my now wet pussy lips. She alternated, licking, then sucking on my clit. I almost reached a peak when she came back and asked me to do the same with her. Before she lay down on the floor, she took two beautiful dildos from her nightstand, one larger than the other. She asked me to lie in 69 position, and I bit my lip before I tasted a woman's pussy for the first time. While I was experiencing how nice her pussy was, she played with the dildos. She held the big one against my pussy, the smaller one against my asshole. I felt how that big dildo was entering my wet pussy. The smaller but violently vibrating vibrator, she now pressed against my clit. I did not like this; it made me crazy. For the first time in my life, I was cumming at the hands of another woman. I had never succeeded, even though I had tried it many times, but I squirted when I came.

She licked me as my orgasm subsided, and I lay down on my back. Brittany sat down with her cunt on my face and made circular movements with my tongue. Still enjoying my orgasm, I licked as if my life depended on it. I felt Brittany's climax building as she rocked her hips on my face, and as she came, she grabbed my hair and pulled my face deeper into her cunt. She came to lie next to me, and we kissed each other — little kisses, then French kisses. Her hand slid back to my pussy, and she fingered me, making me catch my breath. It was clear that a woman knows much better how and where to hit the sensitive chord than a man. I enjoyed it incredibly. Her tongue just turned around mine as though we had been kissing each other for years. When Brittany alternately went in and out of my pussy with two or three fingers, I had taken that dildo and slowly pushed it in and out of her blissful vagina. Both of us wriggled, and almost at the same time, we both came a second time.

"I'm ready," Brittany called. I was reading a magazine in her pajamas and heard Brittany's voice in the hallway. After the first round of sex we had just had, we had decided to meet Jake at the local bar he would be playing in tonight. Jake was in a band. Moments later, my friend stepped into the living room in only a bathrobe, and her hair wrapped in a towel.

"Since when do you leave the bathroom all wet like that?" I asked. It was a strange feeling going back to acting as though nothing had ever happened when only an hour ago, her pussy was on my lips.

"I thought you promised your parents that it would stay at least a little bit tidy here," I added.

"I know, I know," Brittany replied flippantly.

"I did dry myself," Brittany continued.

"I just wanted to ask if you wanted to do my hair?" She laughed. Brittany had beautiful chestnut hair, with curls that fell down her back. I had often admired Brittany, as did most people who saw her.

She was that magazine type beauty and was always finding herself being chased by people who wanted to date her. I had to admit, after the session we had just experienced, I realized that I had always found her beautiful. She was also one of those admirers. Every time she visited her, she was happy to see that Brittany seemed to smile extra sweetly. I remember at the start of our friendship that I would often spend hours trying to find an outfit for when I was going to see Brittany, hoping that she would suddenly find me equally attractive. I was more classically beautiful, with long blond hair that seemed to catch every ray of sun. Brittany and I had spent a lot of time doing each other's hair. I guess I had always secretly loved that Brittany would always want to sit between my thighs as she styled her hair. I had always enjoyed Brittany's perfect curls through her fingers.

"Okay, come here, sweetie," I said. Brittany laughed and sat down between my thighs on the couch, taking the towel off her head to wipe her hair dry. Because of the amount of hair, it took quite a long time, and I didn't want to hurt her, so I took my time. In the meantime, my movements had caused the robe to slip off Brittany's shoulders, and I could not stop myself from looking over Brittany's shoulder and rest my eyes on Brittany's breasts as they were exposed. She could feel the familiar sensation of her clit beginning to throb.

Gosh, she is just so beautiful, I thought. Even though Brittany's tits were not that big, they did have a beautiful shape. Her nipples were relatively large and beautifully round and pink. I did not try to stop my self from staring at Brittany's gorgeous tits and bit my bottom lip as I tried to keep my breathing steady. That was not easy, because her soft skin was still slightly wet and glittered in the moonlight that shone into the living room.

"So. Your hair is ready," I said after a while, "but you're still kinda wet." I got up from the couch and went into the bathroom before taking down another towel. As I walked back into the living room, Brittany stood and dropped her wet towel on the floor, exposing her naked, toned body to my gaze. Smirking I wrapped the towel around my friend and pulled her in close. I rubbed the warm fluffy material over and between Brittany's breasts. I kept a close eye on Brittany's face to see her reaction. Brittany closed her eyes, put her head back, sighed softly, and pushed her chest forward. This only added to the fire which was building deep within me as I caressed Brittany's breasts with her other hand gently.

Suddenly I stopped and took a step back. I had acted like some predatory guy, the kind that we were both always having to turn down rather aggressively. Brittany noticed the hesitation. She opened her eyes and looked up. I looked back, and suddenly an unprecedented longing flowed through my body. I looked Brittany in her big brown eyes and saw the same desire reflected in them. I saw something else, love. We both smirked and looked toward the ground as we both saw the same emotion reflected in the other's eyes. We saw desire and love suddenly realized how blind we had both been. I bit my bottom lip and stepped forward as Brittany began nodding her head as she reached for me and pulled me into her. She bent her head to kiss me passionately. When our lips met, my heart skipped with happiness. To my surprise, Brittany opened her lips and moved her tongue into my mouth. I answered, passionately by letting my tongue slip by as we kissed as I stroked Brittany's breasts. I felt the nipples stiffen under my fingers. Our kiss lasted a long time before Brittany broke it with a laugh, and her cheeks flushed with excitement.

"I dreamed about this," whispered Brittany. I just smiled and felt that I, too, was blushing.

"You can also try the rest. It's different this time. I'm not mad at you anymore," she continued. To my delight I saw that her eyes reflected the truth of her words. I answered with a kiss. Then I lay Brittany down on the couch and knelt beside it. I gently rubbed the towel over Brittany's body.

"You are so fucking beautiful," I whispered. I ran my fingers across Brittany's beautiful body. Brittany moaned softly and pushed her hips up and her legs slightly apart, wanting me to touch her pussy. I saw Brittany's shaven pussy open like a little flower and showing her pink lips glistening in the sunlight. This girl was very wet! I began to caress Brittany's thighs, teasing her as I stroked my fingers across her pussy gently. Brittany sighed deeply as I slid my finger up and down her slit and kissed her inner thighs.

"Wait," muttered Brittany, "I want to see your body." I grinned. I wriggled out of my pajamas and dropped them on the floor. I enjoyed the way Brittany looked at me. Her gaze made confirmed that although I was ten years older than her, my figure was still in shape. She clearly admired me, and I enjoyed her seeing me in a way she had never seen before. I had a wonderfully slender figure with full breasts and blond pubic hair that formed a beautiful, small triangle between her lush thighs. The last time we had fucked it was a power thing, it was different now. Now it was soft and loving, and I was surprised at how my heart melted.

I knelt again and ran my hands down Brittany's body. Over Brittany's shoulders, breasts, her belly and between her legs. Brittany moaned under the tickling and as she reached for my breasts to gently squeeze them. I ran my fingers back over Brittany's pussy and listened to her faltering breath. I used my fingers to open Brittany's pussy and licked her clit with the tip of my tongue. Then I folded the end of my hair into a bun and gently stroked Brittany's soft lips.

Brittany let out a little scream and pushed her hips up, and with it, my head deeper inside. I released my bun and felt my hair tumble back down my back as I flicked it to one side. When I pulled my fingers out of Brittany's tight pussy, she moaned loudly, pulling me close. I stood over her and placed my pussy against Brittany's, who was already wet with her juices. Brittany's gasped as I began grinding my pussy on top of Brittany's, causing her to buck back as she closed her eyes and moaned. Brittany wrapped her arms around my thighs as we rubbed our pussies together with a feverish intensity. My big tits pressed into Brittany's smaller breasts, her nipples getting rock hard. I threw my head back when I felt my intense orgasm take over control of my body. I moaned and growled while Brittany took her breasts and played with them firmly. It wasn't long before Brittany too was writhing in orgasm, her youthful body jerking between my thighs. I leaned over and held her tightly and kissed her fervently, smothering the howling sounds Brittany produced. When I let her go, Brittany was still shaking with the intense experience she had just experienced. I stroked her face and helped her to her feet. We sat side by side on the couch for a while, stroking each other's hair, kissing and whispering sweet words to each other. We stayed like that as the night grew late, and the stars came across the sky. I held Brittany in my arms and knew that whatever happened in the future, she would always have my heart.

Stella and Alexa

Hello, my name is Stella. I have been working for the police for quite a number of years. In my free time, I like to walk through the center of the city. One particular day, after a hard shift, I was going for one such walk. It was a gloomy spring day, and I felt a bit down. It was late, and it would not be long before the stores closed. That is nevertheless an advantage of my irregular services. I can be outside while others are working. However, I had a feeling of emptiness, a feeling of unsatisfied desire. I was looking for excitement, for pleasure. I couldn't help it. Somehow I need it in the week after my period. It will be the hormones I decided as I walked into the perfume store to buy a new scent. I like to do that. The nose is a very important organ for me. Scents linger long, and they can hold memories longer than you can keep them in mind. I went to the counter and waited for my turn. It was quite busy before the end of the afternoon, but I was grateful that I had the time. I saw a 40-year-old woman standing behind the counter with nice, long, red hair. She had something vague about her. The moment she approached another customer in the store, I suddenly heard it. An image of memory came over me. It was Alexa! She had become older, a little slimmer, but still had the same voice. A bit soft and but very sultry, almost a whisper of sexual seduction when she spoke, just like 20 years ago.

About 20 years ago, before I worked for the police, I worked in a nursing home. It was very hard work. But that type of hard work gave a certain satisfaction. After all, you helped people who were no longer able to function independently. We did that work with a number of colleagues. I remembered a few names. In addition to Alexa, they were Tiffany, Amanda, Victoria, and Claire. Amanda, the department head, was a true gay and a very sweet woman. Tiffany was the acting head. I remember at the time she was very young, and she was often very critical. Victoria did the regular evening shifts. And Claire was just like me, a young caregiver. Well, Alexa, I had very special memories of that. She was then a girl of about 20 years old, but somehow she seemed older to me. I was only 19 years old at the time. We worked together a lot, and we felt that the well-being of the, mainly older, residents was of great importance. In the breaks, we often sat together while enjoying a cigarette in the sun and then the stories came loose. She told me about her pajama parties. She lived with a friend in the center of the city. According to her stories, pajama parties were regularly organized there. She told me just enough to get me curious. She even invited me to come to such a party. I wanted to in my heart, but my inexperience prevented me. So I said I couldn't. I remember very well that while she told me about the parties, I got pretty excited. When we got up, I only felt that my pussy had gotten quite wet from those stories. On a very hot summer day, it was decided that there should be ice for the entire department. Alexa and I were going to go get it.

"It's so hot, I hate that I sweat," Alexa said. I replied that it was no better for me that it was because of these uniforms we had to wear. I saw Alexa, sitting behind the wheel, lifting up her white apron at the front and waving the fabric, apparently to get cool.

"You know what? Hold the wheel. I need to take this off," Alexa said as she let go of the steering wheel and began unbuttoning her blouse. I bit my bottom lip as I saw her ample cleavage as the cold air from the air conditioning cooled her. I replied by turning my head and looking out the window.

"I think you should do the same, I don't want you passing out in the car or something," Alexa said as she took the steering wheel back. I slightly nodded my head but was unable to bring myself to loosen the buttons of my thick uniform blouse. At that time, I didn't really know what to do with this situation. I felt quite excited, but I was ashamed of it. I decided to give the conversation a different turn and talked about the department. When we got out of the car, I felt that I had wet my pants, I felt so wet. It was almost certainly not just sweat! Shortly after we bought the ice and returned to work I went straight into the showers to cool off before finishing the rest of my shift.

After a few months, I began working in another nursing home and I lost contact with Alexa. I had pushed the memory of her to the back of my mind over the years, but in recent years I even felt sorry for that did not seize the opportunities she offered me. It had taken me years to discover that I was a lesbian, and even more to learn how to enjoy being with another woman. And now, after all these years, I heard Alexa's voice again and recognized her as if no time had passed at all.

I decided to try to seduce her the same way she had tried to seduce me all those years ago. It was my turn, and she asked if she could help me. I knew right away that she didn't recognize me.

"Yes, I would like a good day cream and a nice scent for my friend, but a scent that can excite me," I said with a sparkle in my eye. I saw that she raised her eyebrows slightly. She picked a scent and let me smell a scent stick. It was Chanel's Egoist.

"Take a sample of this first and see if you like it. Does the cream go in the bag like this, or is it a gift?" She said.

"No, I'll take it like that. It's just for me," I said. I decided that I needed to try something else besides just looking at her suggestively.

"Have you not worked in nursing before?" I asked. I saw the surprise on her face.

"Not only in the past, I still do that, why?" Alexa replied, looking up at me with a slight frown.

"Are you Alexa...?" I asked, very embarrassedly.

"Yes, that's me, who are you?" Alexa questioned. I said who I was. She said she could vaguely remember me. I used to be very slim and had brown hair, but now I had put on five kilograms, and had blonde hair, so that was understandable. I thought it was great that I met her again after all these years. I told her that I was working for the police now. She only did night shifts at the nursing home where we both had worked all those years ago.

"I can't lose contact with you again!" She said before writing down her number and passing it to me. She also told me when she had the night shift so if she didn't pick up that she was either working or sleeping. I put the card in my pocket before saying goodbye.

"Really, I am expecting a call, you know!" She called after me making me laugh as I walked out the door.

A few weeks passed. I had noted very carefully in my electronic diary when Alexa had night shifts. At the end of May, it was then, according to my schedule, that we had a night shift together. It was half-past eleven in the evening, and my shift had just begun. We had completed the briefing, and I went to a consulting room to call Alexa. I was pretty tense. I dialed the number and let it ring four times. No answer. An hour later, I tried again. No result. I was really disappointed. At half-past three, I did exactly the same. After ringing once, she answered the phone.

"Hey there," came her sultry voice down the phone. I had finally succeeded. We were in contact. We talked about the past for an hour. We recalled all kinds of memories and practiced with the names we still knew.

"Can't you come by tomorrow night?" She asked. My heart skipped a beat. We agreed that I would call her at half-past eleven the following evening then she would have just finished the first round. She would call back at 1 o'clock at what time she had a break and that I would come by after that.

The next night I was already excited from the start of the night. We could talk to each other in peace. Could she have changed? Would she be just as horny as 20 years ago? I showered and made sure I wore my favorite scent. I decided to put on my black thong. Normally I don't do that under my uniform, but fortunately, I make exceptions. At the stroke of half-past eleven, I called her again. We talked about anything and everything. I suddenly had the guts to start talking about the pajama parties and the fact that I was so sorry that I had never accepted her invitations. The conversation now slowly began to take on a different tone, and we told each other about sexual experiences. I even told very honestly that I had been very excited a few times by her.

"And is your pussy wet now too? She suddenly asked. What else could I do but admit it? Yes, my pussy was indeed wet.

"Mine too. I'm really dipping now," she said. Moments later, the conversation came about having sex between women. Alexa confessed that she had had a sexual relationship with a woman for many years.

"We couldn't get enough of each other," she

declared her enthusiasm. The conversation had excited me so much that I regretted not putting on a panty liner. I even felt that my uniform pants became damp. We hung up, and she promised to call back 1 hour. At 1 am she called back and told me that at half-past two that I should come and see her.

I waited excitedly until half-past two and told the front desk that I needed to talk to a colleague and that I would stay away for an hour. We had enough people on staff, so it wasn't a problem. With a beating heart, I drove to the nursing home that I knew. A lot had been changed and added; I could see that from the outside. I walked into the entrance and waited for Alexa. Less than a minute later, she came and opened the door. I wanted to kiss her right there and then but changed my mind at the last minute. The time of the exciting aprons was over. She was wearing a sort of pantsuit, a white one. The vest fell well over her ass, so I couldn't see what kind of underwear she was wearing. I secretly hoped that she wore a thong as well. She showed me everything. Some things I recognized and others were new. She said that a colleague had just relieved her. We went to her department and sat down in the day room, and Alexa brought me coffee. To my great joy, Alexa went her post and told her colleague that she no longer needed her. The other nurse left, and we were alone in the ward. We sat next to each other in chairs with a handrail.

I was a bit uncomfortable because I wore my gun, baton handcuffs, and two-way radio on my hips.

"Is it okay, sitting down with all that stuff?" Alexa asked as she touched my gun.

"No, it's actually really uncomfortable, with all my toys," I replied.

"Let's see!" She said. I showed her the shackles.

"I think your wrists are too narrow for this," I said. I grabbed her wrists and closed my fingers around to measure. I held them longer than necessary, and she did not pull her arm back. She just looked me in the eye. I felt the tension rise. I also showed her the big shiny black baton.

"Wow, have you ever," Alexa began to say, stopping when I gave her a look before I had to chuckle.

"No, I haven't used it in my pussy," I replied, knowing what she wanted to ask.

"Seems like such a waste. You carrying that big dildo looking thing and never using it," she teased.

"Who knows, maybe I'll get my chance sooner rather than later," I said, happy when she bit her lip and tried to suppress a giggle. The ice was broken. We were at a point where I wanted to be as she suggested sitting a more comfortable location.

We chose a wide 3-seater sofa in the day room and sat down next to each other once more. I felt the warmth from her leg, which had flattered itself against mine, pulling through my pants. I said she had such beautiful skin and at the same time, stroked her hands. I stroked her between her fingers and along her wrists. I went up slowly until I almost ended up under her armpit.

"Mmmm, safe to say, I am quite excited," she said, licking her lips. I said her face was so beautiful and I turned to her.

"Do you want to kiss, even after all this time?" She asked me very directly. I said nothing but pressed my lips to hers. I felt how her mouth immediately opened and how her tongue shot into my mouth like a liberated wild beast. Our tongues had a sort of sham fight with each other. When we let go of each other, I saw the horniness in her eyes.

"Gosh, Alexa, my nipples are getting really hard," she said. I just rolled my eyes as I didn't believe her, but to my great joy, she opened her vest, and I saw her red bra. Her breasts were bigger than mine. She was wearing a push-up bra, so her breasts were pushing out and looking divine. I saw her beautiful cleavage. She lifted her bra, and her breasts were released. I saw the, indeed hard, nipples protruding straight ahead.

They were beautiful pink and contrasted with her white skin. I could not resist and took her left nipple between my thumb and forefinger. I played with her nipples until I heard her moan. She said she had super sensitive nipples, and I took her nipples into my mouth one by one and sucked them in. I turned my tongue around the areola.

"Jesus, I am soaking wet. I want more!" she cried. I was well aware of the fact that we were in the day-care center of a nursing home and I told her that too. She said, there is an electronic lock on the door, and you can hear those beeps very well. In the meantime, she went into my shirt with her hand. She had loosened a few buttons. She hooked the front of my bra with her index finger. I felt her finger catch on my nipple.

"Mmmm, you also have hard nipples. I think you're also very wet!" She rubbed the crotch of my uniform pants. I had already spread my legs so that she could put her whole hand between my legs. I said that I didn't dare take my pants off because, with all those accessories on, I can't put it back on that easily and suppose someone would come in.

"Then I have it easier," Alexa said, and at once, she tore off her white snaps pants loose. She sat down next to me with a provocative look.

"When I was once in your car with you, you told me you were shaved. How is that now?" I asked, very cheekily.

"Discover it for yourself; I'm not a liar," she said with a smile. At this moment, she looked at the open front of her pants. I was frozen by how beautiful her body looked in her red thong which matched her bra. I hooked my fingers behind the elastic and pulled the fabric down. I moved further and further. I didn't see a single hair. I went into her panties with my hand, and I felt her lovely bald, soaking wet pussy. I kept looking into her eyes, meanwhile letting my right hand continue to go into her slit. I put pressure on my middle finger and pressed it between her labia. I felt her wetness and moved my finger back and forth and curled them inside of her until she moaned and began playing with her clit. Alexa shivered and closed her eyes. I kept going until I heard her growling and felt her cunt muscles contract. I pulled back my hand and licked my fingers.

"I want to feel you too, Stella," she whispered. She released the zipper of my pants and went inside with her hand. This was not easy, because it was a tight pair of pants. At least she managed to reach my pussy, and her slender fingers pressed into my pussy. It hurt a bit, but the excitement won. She was now fucking me with her two wet fingers. I heard it buzz. I didn't last long; I felt that. I tightened all my muscles and tried to postpone my orgasm. It entered the tunnel-like a thunderous train. I could no longer keep still and gave loud cries.

"Sst!" Alexa said, putting a hand on my mouth.

I saw that it was almost 4 o'clock again. I had to go back. I was very sorry, and Alexa also said she was sorry, but her round had to be done. We prepared our clothes, and she explained how I could leave the building without anyone seeing me. I went outside, and I smelled the car again on my right. I smelled the smell of my red-haired girlfriend, and I enjoyed it.

I didn't do much that night. When I was in bed at home after my night shift, I fingered myself with the thoughts of this exciting night shift, and I came incredibly nice again. I think I'll call the next night shift again.

Jasmine and Tiffany

Jasmine suddenly called yesterday. I sat back and watched the TV on the umpteenth heat of a singing show when my phone rang.

"Hey, sweet thing, long time no see." I heard on the other side of the line and immediately knew it was her.

"Far too long," I replied, "it is high time we catch up or something."

"Only talking, or are you in the mood for something else?" Jasmine replied with a smirk in her voice.

"I am in favor of everything," I replied.

"Nice," said Jasmine, "I just got out of the shower, so I'll pull something easy on and grab a nice bottle of wine for you," she said.

"If you prepare the glasses, you will see me in fifteen minutes." Jasmine didn't even wait for my answer because I heard that she was already clicking away from the phone. I quickly jumped in the shower to freshen up and put on a sexy black lingerie set with black stockings. I quickly looked in the mirror, and when I saw myself, I already got the first shiver. I felt like fucking her tonight and felt sexy and horny. I hadn't seen Jasmine in a while, and our last hook up was a few months ago. At the thought of the wonderful mature body of Jasmine, I already felt her experienced hands caress over my body to pamper all my sensitive spots. Jasmine is over 20 years older than me, but she still looked great, and she knew how to spoil both men and women like no other. She had amazing soft breasts with delicious nipples, a slender waist with a full ass and her shaved pussy is great to lick her long lips were great to take in your mouth — the idea that she would be with me again soon excited me a lot and I was just thinking about what kind of exciting things we would undertake this time when the doorbell rang.

I opened the door, and there stood Jasmine in a

long raincoat in front of me. I had not yet closed the door, and she took off her coat and stood in front of me in only a hot pink lingerie set that made me swallow hard and close the door quickly. She had light make-up on with a little silver eye shadow and nude lipstick and painted her nails baby pink. She looked beautiful and sexy and I didn't know whether it was due to the cold or something else, but her nipples were already sticking through the light fabric of her bra. She went straight to the bedroom, and in passing, she gave me a fleeting kiss on my mouth. She took the wine glasses, poured the wine and patted the bed with her hand.

"Come on, take off your pants and sit next to me," she commanded.

"I want to feel your body against mine, baby girl," she added.

"You don't waste any time do you," I said and quickly pulled off my pants to comply with her request. We both took a few sips from our glass of wine, and Jasmine immediately started pulling off my lace blouse. She stroked my arms and kissed me on the neck, and she kneeled on her knees behind me. She unhooked my bra at the back, and I felt her hands slide up over my belly, over my breasts, and she lifted my bra up. Her warm hands stroked my breasts and my nipples, and I closed my eyes and leaned back to find support against her body. I felt my body relax when my bare back touched her chest, and her hands continued to caress my breasts and stomach.

"I missed you," I said, but it was more of a moan than a sentence. Jasmine had grabbed both of my nipples between her thumb and forefingers and began to pull them very gently as I felt her tongue sliding down my neck.

"Please," I moaned, "please be gentle. My nipples, they are super sensitive," I whispered. The pulling on my nipples stopped, and I felt my bra pushed over my arms. I collapsed a little further and now rested myself completely into Jasmine's lap. Her hands stroked my neck and touched my swollen nipples again, her hands slowly slid over my belly, along my panties, and between my thighs. I felt her hands press between my thighs, and my legs were pulled apart, and I was now lying wide apart. Jasmine pushed her hands up my stomach again over my panties and felt her fingers again, touching my nipples. I felt the soft pulling sensation on both my nipples twitching through my body. My nipples were now swollen and red. Jasmine's gentle pulling movements were rhythmic and tender, and it seemed that everything she did to my nipples I could feel in my clit. As a woman, Jasmine knew exactly which sensations would take my body over the edge. I now started moving my hips in time with her touch. I wanted to put my hand between my legs and let my fingers circulate in my wet slit, looking for that small but oh so sensitive place. I felt that Jasmine's hands let go of my nipples, and her hands found their way to my panties making me shiver against her touch.

I had to raise my legs a little, and with an

experienced movement, she pulled my panties away from under my ass and pushed them over my knees to my feet and finally pulled it out over my feet. With my panties in her hands, she tickled my nipples with the bow at the front. It was an exciting sight to see another woman hold my lingerie and touch my nipples with it. We both laughed, and I stuck out my tongue. Jasmine did the same, and the points of our tongues touched gently. Our tongues slowly turned around each other, and I felt them slowly put her tongue in my mouth. I felt her lips on mine and her tongue on the inside of my cheeks. The soft fabric of my panties still tickled my nipples. I felt that I had become quite wet because I felt the first drips of my pussy juices run out and onto my thigh. I spread my legs back as far as I could and felt wonderfully shamelessly lying on the bed.

Jasmine threw my panties on the floor, and her hands stroked my thighs, and for the first time, I felt her fingers go down to my wet lips. We stopped with our tongue kiss, and both looked down at how Jasmine's fingers pulled out my pussy lips. Gently, but as far as it was possible, she pulled my lips aside, and the soft pink flesh of the entrance to my pussy was visible. I tightened my cunt muscles a few times and my clit pulsed few times. I wanted to be fucked. My body was on fire for her. We both enjoyed the view, and Jasmine crawled around my face just before my yearning vagina. Her fingers picked up my nipples again, and where I expected another gentle pulling movement, she put her nails in my sensitive flesh and squeezed hard. I was startled, gave a shout, and then felt my labia being sucked through her warm mouth and trying to penetrate her soft tongue into me.

The pain in my nipples changed into a warm, blissful feeling. I threw my head back and started breathing harder.

"Go on, go on," I moaned and spread my legs to feel as much of her tongue as possible in my cunt. Again her nails squeezed hard in my nipples, and a new burning flood rippled through my nipples to my belly. The burning sensation in my nipples no longer stopped, and Jasmine's tongue had found my clit. A few times, I jerked and moaned uncontrollably. Soon I was able to keep up with the pace of her tongue and pushed my body back and forth on the bed to the rhythm that Jasmine's tongue directed me. Jasmine once again pressed her nails deep into the flesh of my nipples and then released one hand. I felt a finger sliding under her tongue and starting to work on the inside of my wet cunt. I felt her finger penetrate deeper and deeper into me and because it slid in so easily, a second and a third finger soon followed. I felt Jasmine's fingers working my pussy, and I was getting wetter and wetter. Her tongue tirelessly worked on my clit, and the warmth from her mouth mixed with my juices. The first sopping sounds were audible between my legs, and I saw Jasmine take her fingers out of me. She put her four fingers straight ahead and her thumb up, and I felt her hand slide easily into her thumb.

I didn't know I was that wide from below, but the feeling was wonderful. I carefully moved my lower body back and forth and raised myself. It was an intense feeling to ride on Jasmine's hand, and I felt that my first orgasm presented itself. I asked myself if I could have her whole hand, and if Jasmine could read her thoughts, she asked, "Shall we try if you can ride my fist? Have you ever done that?" I didn't answer, but I wanted to try it. Jasmine raised my knees a bit and asked me to relax. That was not so difficult because I wanted so badly to have her whole arm in me and feel her fingers inside me as deeply as possible.

Jasmine put her thumb to her fingers and slowly turned her hand around the entrance to my pussy. I felt the pressure increase, and her hand slide a little further into me. Slowly I was stretched, and the resistance increased as her thumb penetrated further.

"Just a little bit, more, baby," Jasmine said excitedly. Apparently, it was also a new experience for her because she was completely fixated on her disappearing hand between my legs. I tilted my pelvis again, and with a little extra pressure on her hand, Jasmine shot completely into my cunt with a popping sound. A fierce pain broke through my pelvis, and my lower back and the tears shot into my eyes.

"Wait, wait," I shouted, feeling like I was breaking up. Through my tears, I looked down and saw that the hand and a part of her forearm were completely swallowed and disappeared in my cunt. Jasmine started to massage my nipples one by one with her other hand, and slowly, the pain gave way to a burning sensation deep in my lower abdomen. It started on the outside of my cleft where my lips were pressed far out by Jasmine's arm, the sensation pulled in and spread from my left hip to right hip and felt it radiate into my tailbone and ass. Because of the pull on my nipple, the wave flowed upwards to end up in my nipples. I relaxed and felt Jasmine moving her arm back and forth very slowly. I tried to move with her, and to my surprise; I noticed that it was easy. I watched her arm disappear into my cunt more and more and now set the pace myself. After a short while, her arm was so far inside of me that she could go no further. With long strokes, I now started to prepare her hand and swelled the sensation in my belly.

"Please don't stop," I moaned.

"Deeper and harder," I moaned and screamed and whipped myself up to orgasm, submitted all the enthusiasm. Moaning in pleasure and groaning with pain and pleasure, I came to an unprecedented orgasm. I felt it didn't stop, and with an elongated scream, I lifted myself up to once again to fuck Jasmine's arm. Exhausted and crying with emotion, I fell back on the bed, and Jasmine carefully lifted her arm out of my pussy, careful not to hurt me.

Exhausted, I fell into her arms and had to recover for a few minutes. After a few minutes, Jasmine started kissing me, and I felt her tongue nestle again between my pussy lips. I was still panting from my last orgasm, but it was not long before I felt the first sighs of another orgasm. I decided that I needed more time than she was going to give me, so I crawled over Jasmine and took off her soaked pink panties. I had never seen her so wet before. Fisting me had made her insanely horny. I placed my mouth over her pussy and tasted her juices. What a wonderful feeling is that to feel the juices of a woman go through your mouth.

"Lick me, baby," Jasmine whispered, "I am horny, and I have brought something that I think you'll love." I always thought it was wonderful when Jasmine started talking dirty and knew that it meant that she was going to be coming very soon. I worked her slit from top to bottom with my tongue, licked her clit and sucked her lips into my mouth as far as possible and slid further down with my tongue. Her lips swelled in my mouth, and I tasted that she was dripping with excitement. I lifted her legs a little further so that she also lifted her ass up into the air. My tongue slid over her throbbing clit and with the point of my tongue, I pressed into her until I heard her moan. I worked both holes with slow but long strokes, as Jasmine moaned and played with her tits.

I kissed her ass cheeks, biting into her soft but toned flesh and pushed my tongue further into her, slid my tongue through her wet lips, sucked her in as far as possible, and played with her clit. Occasionally I stopped and let my saliva drip from my mouth into her slit. Without taking my mouth off her, I opened my bedside table and removed my sets of nipple clamps. Two metal pegs, the size of my little finger, were connected with a silver-colored heavy chain. I squeezed one of the pegs and carefully placed the serrated edges against Jasmine's swollen nipple. With my mouth, I now quickly moved my tongue back and forth. Jasmine began to moan violently, and I slowly released the pressure on the squeezer so that the cartels squeezed slowly but deeply into her fleshy nipple. There was a deep growl from Jasmine's throat as the pain broke through her chest. Without waiting, I repeated the process with the other squeezer on her other nipple. Her nipples were now connected with a heavy chain, and I could now hurt both her nipples by pulling on the chain with one hand. Moaning with pain and pleasure, I felt Jasmine's body wiggle beneath me, and grunts came from her throat. With my free hand, I slipped a finger into her warm pussy and began curling my fingers inside of her to find her G-spot. A second finger pressed gently against her ass. The abundant presence of saliva and pussy juices between her ass worked great as a lubricant, and my finger slid into her ass very easily. With controlled movements, I penetrated both of her fuck holes while my tongue circled around her clit which drove Jasmine crazy. The panting of Jasmine's body slowly turned into violent shakes. With each shake, her nipples continued to be pulled, and my fingers shot deeper into both her holes.

"I'm going to come. I'm going to come," shouted Jasmine, and I felt her cunt muscles contract violently and quickly. An elongated loud moan her squirting orgasm, and I felt how one spray after the other was sprayed into my mouth and over my face. Jasmine, like no other woman, could come squirting and dripping my hair and face with the moisture that still hit me in rays. It was a wonderful feeling to see the warm moisture squirt from her body and to feel it flow over me. At first, I felt her body tighten completely to relax slowly after thirty seconds. I let my fingers slide out of her and crawled close to her sweaty body. As if she had just taken ten flights of stairs, Jasmine was lying panting and sweating beside me.

I thoroughly enjoyed her orgasm and her after-shocking body. We pressed our bodies tightly together, and our lips found each other. Our bodies had become smooth through all body juices, and we glided wonderfully over each other, our tongues entwined in a fierce embrace. We remained in this close embrace for minutes, until Jasmine got up and pulled a large long dildo out of her bag. I had seen them online before, but seeing one in real life had never happened. Jasmine sat down opposite me and took one end of the dildo in her mouth and brought the other end to my mouth. We both started to suck it slowly and looked at each other in the eye. With one hand around the dildo, I moved my other hand to my soaking wet cunt and began to play with myself. Jasmine did the same and while we looked deep into each other's eyes and the cock continued in our mouths, we fingered ourselves to a second orgasm. It was a new experience for me to masturbate while I continued to look into the eyes of another woman, our mouths connected by a dildo. Almost simultaneously, our orgasm hit, and with a laugh, we removed the dildo from our mouths and placed it in front of our pussies. We both turned a little on our side, both in a different direction, and I slid one leg under Jasmine's and one leg over her other leg. With small jerks, we crawled towards each other, and despite the length of the dildo, we soon worked all the way inside until our pussies touched each other. It was an exciting sight to see our pussies bump into each other.

Only occasionally was the large long dildo visible between us. We glided past each other when we were kissing, and we tried to rub our clits on each other as much as possible. With the large dildo deep in our cunts, we worked ourselves to a third orgasm. With wild movements and loud moans, we came together and let ourselves fall exhausted, the dildo still stabbing into our pussies. Exhausted, we stayed at least 10 minutes before we moved close to each other and fell into an extremely satisfying sleep. It had become an unexpected evening, but certainly, one that was worth repeating. In any case, we agreed that next time, we would not wait months before seeing each other again.

Luna and Grace

Luna had been working in the same café for three years. It wasn't that it was a bad job; it was just that her mind craved something more. The problem was, not many companies were happy to take on someone straight out of jail. Maybe if that was her only setback, they could overlook it, but it wasn't. Luna had bounced from foster care home to foster care home to the streets during her youth. A series of break-ins had caused her to be sent to juvenile detention, and once released, an armed robbery had sent her to jail. Now 23, Luna was considered an adult by everyone who saw her, but she had never actually grown up. She had merely survived and aged.

So although she desperately craved something more mentally stimulating, she stayed put for the steady paycheck and stability of the routine.

It was a busy Saturday morning. Luna worked six days a week, she liked that it kept her busy, so she knew all the regular customers, but on this particularly busy day, she saw a woman who she had wished never to see again.

"Just a black coffee, thanks," the tall and glamorous woman said without looking at Luna. Luna waited until the woman looked up before she spoke, glaring her down in a way her regulars had not seen before.

"And maybe an apology for being such a bitch?" Luna said before she could stop herself. She clutched the counter so tightly her knuckles turned white as her manage heard the words she said and quickly rushed over to the women.

"Sorry, Ma'am, I'll be taking over here," Luna's manager said as she placed her hands on Luna's shoulders and turned her towards the back room.

"Go cool down," she whispered into Luna's ear and gently pushed her into the direction of the back.

Luna stayed out the back for the rest of her shift, angrily pacing back and forth. She liked that her boss didn't try to talk to her or try to calm her down. She just let her stay there until the day was over, and the store was closed. When she came into the back room, she saw Luna still had the look of murder in her eyes, and she sighed.

"Luna, come here, sweetie," her manager said as she opened her arms to Luna, who reluctantly walked into the embrace and let the older woman hold her.

"Do you want to tell me who that was?" Her manager asked as Luna fought back her tears and shook her head.

"Ok. I'm worried about you being alone tonight, and it's your day off tomorrow. I'm worried about what you'll do with all that free time. How about you come and stay with me for a few days?" Her manager suggested. Luna just shrugged her shoulders before nodding her head slowly.

"Thanks, Grace," Luna softly said as she followed Grace out of the back room and into the night.

Grace's house was only a short stroll from the café, and she watched as Luna wrapped her coat around her small frame, trying to keep warm. Winter had come early this year, and the cold weather had not been kind to Grace's staff, who had all come down with the flu, everyone except for Luna, who had worked double shifts the previous week.

"Hey, I never got the chance to really thank you for all your work last week. How about I take you to dinner as a thank you. I would have been lost without you," Grace suggested. Luna just shrugged her shoulders, which Grace had learned meant, yes. Grace smiled and took Luna's cold hand in her warmer, glove covered ones and walked them into a diner she knew Luna would love.

In the three years Grace had known Luna, she had managed to find three things about her. The first was that the girl could eat! If she had the option of burgers, fries, and pancakes, she would choose it every time over going to a fancy restaurant. The second was that even though she didn't speak very much outside of her customer service, she watched everything and could read people incredibly well. And the third was that she was a lesbian. The last one excited Grace the most. Mostly because Grace was also gay, and even though she could have a different girl every night, she had found that the most rewarding relationships were with the girls who she had to work really hard for.

Grace was 33 years old and had been managing the café for five years. She had long, thick chestnut curls that looked as imposing as a lions mane. Her hourglass frame caught the attention of most men, and certainly, a large number of women and the energy she exuded was a mix between confidence, certainty, and power. That was what Luna had been attracted to the moment she had met Grace.

"We are here, honey," Grace said as they

turned the corner and walked toward the diner door. Luna let out a small chuckle when she saw where they were headed.

"Did you know it was my favorite?" Luna asked, pulling her hand away from Grace's and putting both hands into her pockets.

"I may have pieced it together over the years," Grace said, winking at Luna, who just gave off a sideward smirk. They walked inside, and Luna made a beeline for her favorite booth, right at the back where she could see everyone coming and going. After ordering two cheeseburgers, fries, extra-large chocolate and a stack of buttermilk pancakes, Luna sat back and brought her knees to her chest and looked out the window. Grace had ordered the French toast and a black coffee and watched as Luna's eyes flittered across all the people who passed the window.

"The woman there today, the one I lost it at. She was the medic at the detention center I was in," Luna said, still looking out the window. Grace's coffee came, and she sipped the warm liquid as she watched Luna.

"I see," she replied, unsure of what to say and not wanting to push Luna's buttons on the subject.

"Well, I doubt she will be coming back. You did a good job of not punching her in the face," Grace added, making Luna smile and turn to face her as her meal was set out in front of her.

"Are you really going to eat all that?" Grace teased, making Luna smile and again and sigh in relaxation.

"Yes," came her simple reply as she began to cut her pancakes elegantly.

"She would do stuff like tell us we had to have a full body check and have us handcuffed to the bed and then fuck us. The guards fucking knew too, but I guess she had something on them or something coz they knew did shit," Luna said between mouthfuls of fluffy pancakes. Grace frowned and shook her head.

"I don't even think she liked women, I think it was just a power thing," Luna said, detaching herself from the experience. Grace finished her French toast as Luna moved onto her first burger.

"I'm sorry that happened to you, sweetie," Grace said, the affection in her voice catching Luna off guard.

"Why do you care?" Luna asked out of genuine confusion.

"Why do I care? Because that is not what normal people do to someone else. Especially someone who is meant to be looking after someone. You were right. She's a fucking bitch," Grace replied, making Luna laugh.

"I've never heard you swear before," she said as she sipped on her shake.

"Well, there is a time and a place for everything, darling," Grace said, eyeing the fries on Luna's plate.

"You can have some. This isn't jail. I'm not going to cut you for taking my food," Luna said, making Grace laugh.

"Here," Luna insisted, pushing the plate toward Grace.

"No one has ever said that I was right before. Or even believe me," Luna said, breaking Grace's heart.

"Well, I believe you, sweetie. And you were right to do what you did today. If I had known, I would have kicked her out the moment she set foot in my store," Grace said as Luna finished her second burger.

"I might get these to go," Luna said as she saw snow beginning to fall onto the sidewalk. Grace nodded, and they made their way to her house.

Luna was surprised by how spacious Grace's house was, considering it was in the middle of town.

"Well, I actually bought two run-down hotels, knocked them down, and then build my house on the land, it was just easier to do it that way," Grace explained.

"Wasn't that super expensive?" Luna asked, looking over Grace's modern living space.

"Um, I suppose," Grace said, shrugging her shoulders. Luna had always wondered what Grace's motivation was for working in the café. It had been clear from the first day they had met each other, that Grace had money. Luna just had never put too much thought into it, but seeing how Grace lived, in the center of the city in luxury, spacious home, Luna knew that it must be generational.

"Anyway, I have a spare room this way if you want to have a look," Grace said, leading Luna into a room that was as big as her entire apartment. Luna just nodded.

"Yeah, I mean, it's ok, I guess," she teased, making Grace laugh.

"There's a bathroom that way if you'd like to take a shower and there's clean pajama's in the top drawer as well as a robe and slippers. If you need anything, my room is just on the other side," Grace said to a slightly bewildered Luna.

"Ok, thanks," Luna said softly, making Grace smile.

"Ok. Goodnight," Grace said, clapping her hands together and shutting the door behind her as she left.

"Woah," Luna said out loud when Grace had left. She took in the high ceilings of the room, the view of the green space out of the floor to ceiling folding French doors. She shook her head and walked into the modern bathroom. She stripped off and let her clothes drop onto the floor before walking into the shower and pressing the buttons until she figured out how to make warm water come from the rainwater shower head. She used the body wash and shampoo and conditioner that was in the shower and enjoyed the luxury smelling products she had never even heard the name of. Drying herself on the fluffy white towel that was warm from the heated towel rack. Sighing in relaxation, Luna made her way to the comfortable king-size bed in the middle of the room and collapsed, full from her dinner and exhausted from the emotional day she had no desire to relive.

Luna woke to the sound of chilled house music coming from what she assumed to be the kitchen. She blinked her eyes open and looked around the room. The sun was pouring in through the windows, and she yawned as she stretched before getting out of bed. She slipped her feet into the navy blue slippers, found the matching satin robe and wrapped it around her body. Walking out into the open space of the kitchen and living room, Luna saw Grace and smiled as she saw the bacon and eggs she was making.

"Hey," Luna said sheepishly before sitting down on the couch.

"Hi sweetheart. Hungry?" Grace asked to Luna, who just nodded her head. Luna reached forward to pick up a magazine and flicked through the pages before putting it down again.

"Thanks for letting me stay. I really love it here," she said as she saw Grace begin to plate up their breakfast.

"It is my pleasure. I am really happy that you took me up on my offer. I love it here, but sometimes it does get a bit lonely," Grace said as she placed a green tea in front of Luna.

"I don't know. You could always hire a girl for the night," Luna laughed in the cheeky way that Grace had fallen in love with. This is the Luna she enjoyed having round, the calm and relaxed one who wasn't afraid of the world. This side of Luna was a rarity to see, but as her blonde hair fell out from behind her ear, Grace knew that it was something worth treasuring.

"I have taken the day off as well. I thought it might be nice to go for an outing or something. What do you think?" Grace asked as Luna ate her breakfast.

"As long as we get frozen yogurt after, I don't care what we do," Luna said, sipping the tea. Grace smiled as her cat sauntered inside.

"Hi Cherry," Grace said, smiling at how excited Luna was by her presence.

"I didn't know you had a cat!" Luna exclaimed.

"There are a few things you don't know

about me," Grace muttered to herself, but Luna had heard.

"Um, I know you think I'm pretty," Luna said, causing Grace to swiftly turn to face her, her face beginning to turn red. Luna got up slowly, her eyes changing into the seductress she knew she could be.

"What? Was it meant to be a secret?" Luna teased. Grace just sighed.

"That's not why I invited you over Luna," Grace said, feeding the cat before walking over to the couch and sitting down.

"I know. I wouldn't have come if it was. I think it's sweet you never tried anything," Luna said, sitting next to her and placing her hand on Grace's thigh.

"But, I think it might be nice," Luna said, shrugging her shoulder and looking at Grace, who was clearly struggling with the idea.

"But I'm not like that. I don't want to just have sex with you for the sake of having sex with you. I think you're more special than that," Grace said, wrapping her arm around Luna's body and pulling her in tight. Luna loved how it felt to have Grace's arms around her body and lifted herself up and onto Grace's lap.

"Luna. I don't want you to feel like I am taking advantage of you or something. You might not see it, but I can," Grace said, making Luna roll her eyes.

"Please shut up," Luna said softly before kissing Grace full on her lips. Grace moaned into the kiss and wrapped her arms around Luna's body tighter.

"Oh my god, baby," Grace said as she stood up, still holding onto Luna's body before placing her on her back on the couch. Grace dropped her body on top of Luna's and pressed her thigh against Luna's pajama covered pussy making Luna begin to grind on her.

"You're so fucking beautiful," Grace said as she watched Luna rub her pussy against her thigh while stroking her forehead.

"I want you," Luna almost whimpered,

causing Grace to lower herself back on top of Luna's smaller frame and hold onto her as she continued to grind on Grace's thigh.

"Take what you need, sweetie," Grace said, placing a hand on Luna's ass before grabbing at her.

"It's not working," Luna said angrily before getting up and pushing Grace away. She brought her knees to her chest and frowned as she tried to hold her tears back.

"It's ok honey. Come here," Grace said, opening her arms to Luna and wrapping them around her.

"I still want you around," she added as Luna rested in her arms. Grace held her until she relaxed and stop breathing shallowly.

"Can we try it like this, maybe?" Grace said as she took Luna's hand in hers and led her to the spare room Luna had slept in the previous evening. Grace smiled as she twirled Luna and then pushed her down onto the bed.

"Take your clothes off," Grace said making

Luna bite her bottom lip.

"I'm waiting," Grace added, getting a smile from Luna, who began to obey.

"Pretty girl," Grace said once Luna was naked in her bed. Grace came and lay next to Luna, who began to pull at her pajamas.

"No baby," Grace lovingly said causing Luna to look up her with her big eyes.

"Why not?" Luna asked as she was held.

"Because we are trying something," Grace explained as she ran her fingers down Luna's back, giving her goosebumps and causing her to rock her hips in time Grace's touch.

"What are we trying? Being bored?" Luna teased. Grace loved the cheeky look in Luna's eyes and kissed her forehead.

"Something like that," Grace replied, not taking the bait.

"I want you to close your eyes, sweetie," Grace said as she felt Luna begin to try and overpower her. Reluctantly, Luna closed her eyes and bit her bottom lip in anticipation.

"Good girl," Grace said as she began to kiss Luna's cheek and down her neck. A slight moan escaped her lips and caused her to open her eyes suddenly.

"Did you feel that?" Grace asked already knowing the answer. Luna just nodded her head and snuggled back into Grace's embrace as the older woman tenderly touched and kissed her body.

"Let me if you want to stop," Grace said as she felt Luna's back muscles flex under her touch and pull her tighter into her body. Grace held Luna in her arm as she snaked the other one down her body and let it rest above Luna's pussy. Kissing her, Grace felt Luna moan into her mouth as she spread her thighs and gently patted Luna's pussy.

"Can I, baby girl?" Grace asked and waited for Luna to open her eyes. Grace smiled down on Luna, who looked beautifully innocent and vulnerable in her arms as she slowly nodded yes.

"I'll be gentle, tell me if you want to stop," Grace said as she parted Luna's pussy lips and felt her wet slit. Gasping, Luna tensed her body, and Grace stroked her up and down until she relaxed once more in her arm.

"There you go. Good girl," Grace said as she rubbed over Luna's clit, causing her to roll her head back and close her eyes. Luna's breaths began to come in short, shallow pants as Grace worked her cunt, tensing once more as she felt Grace's fingers at the entrance of her pussy.

"Is this ok?" Grace questioned as Luna rested on her elbows and watched as Grace slowly pushed her fingers into her pussy.

"Yeah," Luna breathlessly gasped as she was filled. Grace waited until Luna's muscles relaxed around her fingers before she began pushing them in and out of Luna's tight pussy.

"So fucking beautiful," Grace said as she felt Luna's pussy begin to gush with juices. She curled her fingers inside of Luna who was moaning and biting her bottom lip as she came in Grace's arms. Panting, Luna pushed Grace off her and looked at her as though she had just answered all her deepest questions.

"What do you think?" Grace asked, a smirk on her face. Luna tried to think, but her thoughts seemed blocked.

"I'm not sure," she quietly said as she got up and walked into the bathroom. Grace thought for moment before getting up and following Luna into the shower.

"We don't have to talk about it if you don't want," Grace said, taking the shower gel and pouring it over her breasts.

"Then why are you talking about it?" Luna asked, trying not to sound as aggressive as she did.

"Here," Grace said passing the gel to Luna, unphased by Luna's apparent emotional detachment. They washed in silence. The only words shared when Luna thanked Grace for passing her a towel.

Luna walked to where she had left her bathrobe and tied it around her waist.

"I put your clothes from yesterday in the washing machine. They'll be ready soon, they are just in the drier now," Grace said, coming to sit next to Luna.

"Look. I know you are just trying to be nice. But you really don't need to," Luna said, admiring how Grace's breasts looked in her robe.

"Oh goddamn Luna, shut up. I know you aren't used to people being nice to you or taking care of you. I know you're so big and tough and can handle yourself, but that doesn't mean that it's the only way to live and if I want to look after you while you are in my house, then that's what I'm going to fucking do," Grace said, making Luna laugh and wrap her arms around her and bite into her shoulder.

"Then why didn't you just say that in the first place," Luna said snuggling into the older woman's body.

"Yeah that's what I fucking thought," Grace said, holding onto Luna and watching as Cherry played with a leaf outside.

"Why do you even want me?" Luna asked as

they made their way to the frozen yogurt store.

"Oh I don't know. I guess I wanted to find the most fucked up girl I could," Grace said, making Luna laugh and reach for her hand.

"But what if I'm not fucked up anymore?" Luna said, making Grace roll her eyes.

"Then I guess I did my job right, princess," Grace said opening the door and holding it open for Luna.

"You're going to make yourself sick eating all that," Grace said, watching as Luna almost overfill her cup with chocolate yogurt.

"Incorrect," Luna happily said as she sprinkled choc-chips over her mountain for chocolate yogurt.

"Cute," Grace said as she saw how Luna happy danced as she waited for her turn to pay.

"Let me?" Grace asked, delighted when Luna nodded her head without hesitation.

"If I had known that you'd be such a great sugar mama, I would have hit you up for it years ago," Luna cheekily said as Grace passed her a pink spoon.

"Oh please, do you remember how angry you were a year ago? You would have never let me near you," Grace teased, taking Luna's hand in hers and leading her back to the car.

"I wasn't angry, I was alert," Luna corrected, licking the spoon seductively.

"Oh, alright," Grace replied, not believing a word of what Luna was saying.

"So, you got your treat. I want mine now," Grace said, placing her hand on Luna's thigh, laughing when Luna pushed her hips forward.

"That is so not what I meant," Grace laughed.

"Weird," Luna said.

"Well, if you are offering," Grace said, a slight questioning in her voice.

"Uh-huh," Luna replied nodding her head. Grace didn't wait for her to change her mind as she pulled Luna's panties to the side and felt her juicy pussy.

"Oh my god. Come on, let's get out of here,

baby girl," Grace said, turning on the ignition and driving out of the parking lot and onto the street.

"Where are we going?" Luna said as Grace drove down to a few back streets and to a beach that Luna had never been to before.

"Just about there," Grace said, beginning to finger Luna's pussy. Luna put her frozen yogurt container down and lifted her hips to allow more of Grace's fingers inside of her.

"That's a good girl," Grace said, stopping the car and pushing her seat back.

"Come here," she said, unclipping Luna's seat belt and pulling her onto her lap, making her straddle her thighs.

"Wrap your arms around my neck," Grace instructed to Luna, who obeyed immediately. Luna rested her body on top of Grace's and loved how she was enveloped in the older woman's body.

"Such a wet little thing," Grace said as she finger fucked Luna, whose thighs were tensing and shaking as she felt her orgasm begin to build inside of her.

"Please don't stop," Luna gasped as she felt Grace's hand on her back, holding her in place.

"I didn't plan on it," Grace said almost to herself as she felt her bicep tense as she fucked Luna. Gasping, Luna lifted off Grace's lap as her orgasm hit her, only to be pushed back down as Grace kept her fingers inside the young girl and made her hold them inside of her as her body was racked with an intense rush. Luna rested her head on Grace's shoulder and whimpered as her juices flowed from her and onto Grace's lap.

"My pretty girl," Grace said, kissing the top of Luna's forehead.

"You know, I would be your sugar mama if you wanted, baby?" Grace said, causing Luna to let out an exhausted laugh.

"I'm going to take that as a yes ok, honey?" Grace said, smiling as Luna shrugged her shoulder and looked up at her with those big eyes, Grace had fallen in love with all those years ago.